Anthony

Harold J. Fischel

ISBN: 1494851210
ISBN 13: 9781494851217
Library of Congress Control Number: 2013923838
CreateSpace Independent Publishing Platform,
North Charleston, South Carolina

*This novel is dedicated to my wife Jan,
for her encouragement and support. But most of all for being
my spelling guru, beta reader, and assisting in the final check
of the edited manuscript.*

Prologue

It was the lead story on every news channel that week. The plane carrying Lieutenant General Bruce (Chip) Walker had exploded on the runway while preparing to take off from a small military facility in Bosnia. The cause of the explosion was never discovered. And the army, while disputing foul play, never officially ruled out sabotage.

Chip Walker was an immensely popular soldier. A West Point graduate, he was well on his way to receiving his fourth star and eventually being appointed Army Chief of Staff. In his younger years, Chip had led the US equestrian team to two Olympic medals. He was married to the Texas socialite Mary McPherson. Three of his children had followed in his footsteps and had been selected to represent the United States in the Olympics, two for jumping and one for the bobsled team.

Chip's death caused quite a stir when the secret provisions of his will leaked out. In his will he designated a considerable sum of money for the benefit of his longtime mistress and her son. In this will he acknowledged that the boy was his son and that he had secretly been supporting Yuni, his mistress. He had helped Yuni immigrate to the United States and had kept her tucked away in an apartment on Central Park West in New York City. Shocked and dismayed by this revelation, Mary, his widow, instructed her lawyers to fight the provisions of the will. The court ruled against her, but the lawyers did manage to secure a ruling that neither Yuni nor the child would have any further claims against the estate.

Aided by the notoriety she gained through all the publicity surrounding the revelation of her secret liaison with the highly respected general, the beautiful Yuni became a top model. At the height of her career, she was featured on the cover of *Vogue* magazine. Mary, her children, and the rest of the McPherson family did their best to separate themselves as far as possible from Yuni and her son, Anthony.

Soon after posing for an extremely popular USO poster, Yuni was diagnosed with bone cancer. For the next two years, she was in and out of hospitals, undergoing severe chemotherapy treatments. She was eventually declared cancer free, but not until after her doctors had been forced to amputate her left leg. The years of medical bills and the expense of hiring an au pair to take care of young Anthony while she was in the hospital ate through her financial reserves and left her with a mountain of unpaid bills. As a freelance model, she did not carry health insurance. She was forced to declare bankruptcy.

I

"Anthony, come in here and help me close this suitcase. Hurry, the movers will be here any minute."

Anthony got up slowly. "All right, already, I'm coming!" He had been lying on the floor in the hallway clutching Zorbo, his shaggy-haired mutt. He got up slowly and went into his mother's bedroom, where she was trying to pack the last of her clothes into a big suitcase lying next to her wheelchair.

"Help me get those sweaters from the top shelf and put them here in the suitcase." Anthony had to stand on his toes to reach the sweaters. Careful not to unfold them, he placed them in the suitcase and turned to his mother.

"Why can't I take Zorbo with us?"

"Anthony, we have been over this many times before. The Housing Authority on Third Avenue won't allow dogs."

"But, Mom, I can't leave him! I won't! I have had him since he was a puppy. Dad gave him to me just before he died."

"I know, baby, I love Zorbo too, but don't make things more difficult for me, please. We are not allowed to bring him to our new apartment. I tried, but they just won't allow dogs. I did the best I could by arranging for the Sanders next door to take him. He knows them, and your friend Timmy will take good care of him."

Anthony burst out crying, and Zorbo ran into the room, wondering what had happened to his young boss. With tears streaming down his face, Anthony tried to explain to his mother. "Timmy told me they'll put him down. They told Timmy it's a shame; Zorbo is a very nice dog, but they already have Ricky, their golden retriever, and Willow, the cat. They can't have another dog in the apartment." Anthony was desperate. "Mom, you can't let them kill Zorbo. Please don't let it happen!"

Before Yuni could respond to her son's anguish, the doorbell rang.

Without waiting for someone to respond to the bell, Pete, the head of the moving crew, barged in. He heard Anthony crying and headed straight for the bedroom.

"What is the matter, young fellow, sad to leave this place?"

Without concern as to whom this man might be, Anthony blurted out, "You have to help, they are going to kill my dog."

"Don't worry, as long as Pete is around, nobody is going to kill any dogs." Yuni assumed this was one of the movers, but she thought she better ask to make sure. "Yes, madam, I'm Pete. Me and my crew will get you all packed up, and we will move you to your new place. If I may ask, what's this killing the kid's dog all about?"

"The place we are moving to won't allow dogs. I have pleaded with them, but the housing authority will not make an exception. There is nothing I can do but leave him here with our neighbors."

"They'll kill him," Anthony screamed.

"Calm down, young man, I told you nobody kills dogs while Pete is around. The housing authority does not have enough people available to check on the condition of the apartments, let alone to check if anyone keeps a dog on the premises. I'll talk to the superintendent in charge of the building you're moving into. I know all those guys; he won't give you any trouble. Besides, there are so many stray dogs around that building complex that nobody will know the difference."

"Really, we can take Zorbo?" The tears disappeared like magic.

"Yes, Zorbo is coming along. And what is your name, young fellow? And what kind of a name is Zorbo?"

"I am Anthony, and Zorbo comes from Zorro and Boy. I thought of it myself when my father brought him home. I was three years old, and Zorbo was three weeks, so we are sort of the same age."

"And how old are you now?"

"I'm ten, almost eleven, sir."

"Well, Anthony, I can see you love that dog, so don't worry. Zorbo will come with me in the big truck, and we'll be waiting for you when you and your mother arrive at your new apartment." Turning to Yuni, Pete apologized for sticking his nose into the issue of taking the dog. Yuni admitted that she had not known how to handle the situation and that she had prayed to find a way to have Anthony have his best friend with him when he moved into his new surroundings.

While the movers packed up her belongings and carted them off via the freight elevator to the moving van parked at the curb, Yuni stayed in her bedroom, feeling miserable. It was left up to Anthony to point out what was going with them and what furniture had been sold and would be picked up later in the day. Before long the au pair arrived. A month before, Yuni had informed her that she could no longer afford her and that she would have to let her go. Besides the finances, as a practical matter, it would have been impossible to retain her services. The apartment they were moving into had only one bedroom. That was all Yuni could afford on her disability allotment. She was devastated that Anthony would have to sleep on a couch in the living room.

Anna, the au pair, was as bubbly as ever. She realized Yuni was having a difficult time and did her best to cheer her up.

"Yuni, I am coming along to help you get settled in the new apartment. After the movers have placed the furniture and other heavy things, you direct me, and I'll unpack. Of course, Anthony will help too. I know all this is tough on you, but let's pretend this is a new adventure. After I get you unpacked, we'll go out and explore your new neighborhood. You'll have to know which stores you can get around in and which stores to avoid. I already printed out which bus routes are available to you. Taxis are too expensive."

"Anna, Anna, I truly love you, but you really do not have to do this. I already owe you for the last two months. I promise to pay you, but I can't right now."

"Stop it! I don't want to hear about money. When I spoke to my folks back in Holland and mentioned what a hard time you were having, my father made me promise not to accept any more money from you. I am sure he would disown me if I did. Yuni, don't worry about me. I'm okay, really I am. As you know, I moved in with my friend Betty, and my father promised to fully support me if I wanted to enroll in graduate school this fall. Luckily, I can stay in the United States as long as I want. I was born here. I told you that before. Remember, I was born here while my dad worked for a Dutch bank here in New York."

Yuni could not help but smile. "Yes, I certainly remember how you liked to tease me that you were the native and I was the immigrant. But I did become a citizen as soon as I qualified," she added proudly. "I did that all on my own without the help from the general, and I made sure Anthony would be a citizen too, and that his last name would definitely be Walker and not Abayari like mine."

"Did the general object to that?"

"No, he was devoted to Anthony. I think he stayed with me all those years, even at the risk of our affair becoming public, because he loved Anthony so much. But now, about you. Go on with your life. Don't worry about us; we'll be okay. You're a pretty young girl. Enjoy yourself while you can. Let me give you the one thing I have left that I can give you, and that is some good advice. Don't be any man's mistress, regardless of how much you love him. If he does not want to marry you, send him on his way."

"Yuni, I never heard you like this. You always spoke so highly of the general, but now you sound bitter. Do you regret the years you spent with him?"

"No, I don't. I just hate what I have done to Anthony. No child deserves that. He is the victim of our selfishness. We only thought about our own desires and never considered his future."

The conversation had taken Anna off guard, and she did not know how to respond. During the past two years, she had become Yuni's close friend and confidante. She was one of the few who knew the true identity of the mysterious man, generally assumed to be Yuni's husband, who traveled all over the world for his oil drilling business. She had always assumed that because of Yuni's deep love for the general, which she was sure was mutual, that Yuni had no regrets. Anna needed some time to think about the feelings Yuni had just revealed for the first time. She stood up and pushed her long blond hair away from her face.

"I'll take Anthony and Zorbo for a walk. Mind if we leave you alone with the movers?"

"No, go ahead. Anthony can use some fresh air, and I think Zorbo has not been out since early this morning."

After Anna and Anthony had left with the dog, Yuni remained in her bedroom. The movers were working in the guest room adjacent to her bedroom, and she could clearly hear their conversation. The young good-looking fellow was the loudest of the crew.

"Hey, Pete, don't you think that lady in the wheelchair looks a little like that Eurasian model who was so popular a few years ago? If I recall correctly, her name was Yuni something or other. Man, I tell you, she was something else. What a piece!"

"Shut up, Josh, you're being very rude." The conversation continued in hushed tones, and Yuni could hardly discern their whispers. A few moments later, Pete entered her bedroom. "Sorry about that remark, but Josh meant no disrespect. My guys really admire you. When I told them that Josh was right and that you are indeed the famous model, I had to hold them back to keep them from bursting in here to ask for your autograph."

"That's okay. I am not offended; it's nice to know they remember me from my better days."

"Am I out of line if I ask if you had a car accident or something? The guys mentioned that they had not heard anything about you in the past couple of years, and we were just wondering."

"I only wish it was a car accident. No, I lost my leg to cancer."

"Oh my God, I'm so sorry. I really didn't mean to pry into your personal life."

"It's okay, Pete. It's only natural to ask what happened. Cancer is a dreadful disease, and you can see how it can ravage someone. Tell your crew I'm pleased that they remembered me, and I loved Josh's remark. It's the best thing that's happened to me all day."

By the time Anna and Anthony returned, the movers were ready to go. Anna called a cab, and the three of them followed the moving van to the new apartment. Anthony would not get in the cab until he made sure that Zorbo was safely seated next to Pete in the truck.

II

The move to Third Avenue turned out to be even more difficult than Yuni had feared. Most of the projects north of Ninety-Seventh Street were relatively safe, but the building Yuni and Anthony moved into had quite a few unsavory tenants who relished terrorizing their more defenseless neighbors. The 463-unit, 20-story complex, owned and operated by the New York City Housing Authority, had long since been designated as a problem area. Police officers from the department's housing bureau frequently patrolled the premises.

Yuni had been given an apartment on the fourth floor, which was generally considered one of the better floors. But because there were only two of them, they had been assigned a very small apartment. Even though Yuni had gotten rid of most of her furniture, the few pieces she kept did not all fit into her new apartment. Anna and she tried their best, but they could not find a way to fit her two beautiful leather couches with the matching easy chairs into the small living room. She was forced to sell them. The only consolation she had for losing the last of the furniture the general had bought her was that she sold them for much more than she expected. The extra money allowed her to splurge on a new sofa bed for Anthony to sleep on.

Anthony suffered the most from the move. He did not tell Yuni, but from the very beginning, the neighborhood kids taunted him. He was reluctant to leave the apartment and only went outside to walk Zorbo or get something for Yuni from the store. As the first day in his new school approached, he was in a near panic. He did not dare tell his mother, but he feared having to walk the ten blocks to school all by himself. Yuni had taken him there to register for the new school year, and she was happy that the school was close enough for him to walk by himself. The night before the first school day, he lay awake most of the night. He hardly touched his breakfast. Yuni considered this quite normal. After all, he was going to a new school for the first time. She never suspected that he was afraid of the walk.

Anthony kissed his mother good-bye and bravely left for school. He was so concerned about the walk to school that he failed to notice that Zorbo slipped out the door right behind him. The elevator was crowded with adults, and it was not until he was halfway to the school that he encountered the first group of kids. The taunting started immediately.

"Hey, little fruitcake, come over here and show us what your mommy made you for lunch." Pretty soon the whole group joined in. "Yeah, show us what is in that bag, maybe we want to share." Anthony put his head down and kept on walking, trying to ignore them. One of the older boys caught up to him and tried to pull his lunch bag out of his hand. Anthony quickly pulled the bag back and tried to push the kid away.

"Leave me alone. I made my own lunch, and I have to go to school." The boy grabbed his arm and threw him on the ground. This was the first time any of them had attacked him physically. Anthony had no idea what to do; he had never been in a fight before. He covered his head and stayed on the ground. "Please, I didn't do anything to you guys. Leave me alone. I have to go to school." The kid came over and tried to push him flat on the ground with his foot. "Please, leave me alone! I never did anything to you guys. Just take the bag." The boy put his foot on Anthony's neck and pushed his face into the sidewalk.

By now Anthony was desperate. He started to cry, and his voice broke as he once more begged to be left alone. Suddenly a snarling dog threw himself between Anthony and his attacker. It was Zorbo, and he was ready to tear anyone apart who dared harm his master. He stood over Anthony with teeth bared, snarling viciously. The attacker and his friends backed away. They took off in a hurry when they saw that this dog meant business and was ready to do some serious harm.

Anthony did not immediately realize what had happened, and he only recognized it was Zorbo when the dog happily started licking his face. He put both arms around Zorbo's neck. He was so relieved and happy to hold his dog that he could not hold back his tears as he buried his head in the dog's furry neck. As if the dog could answer him, he asked, "Zorbo, how did you get here?"

Anthony got up on his knees and held Zorbo for a moment longer before he stood and retrieved his lunch bag, which the attackers had left behind. Anthony straightened his clothes a little, and the two of them headed for school. Anthony knew he did not have enough time to bring Zorbo home, but he was sure the dog could find his way back if he told him to go home. He never took the dog in the elevator, so he figured Zorbo would go up the staircase and bark at the apartment door to be let in. Anthony hoped that Mr. Zakowsky, the old man who also lived on the fourth floor, would not see Zorbo all by himself in the hall.

From the day they moved in, Mr. Zakowsky complained about having a dog in the building. He tried to get the superintendent to enforce the no-dog rule, and when he could not get him to act, he took to complaining directly to Yuni and Anthony. Whenever he saw Anthony with the dog, he would come up to him and say, "You knuw you kan't haf a dog here. Dat is de rule." Yuni had instructed Anthony to stay polite and just say he would make sure that Zorbo stayed out of the way and never bothered Mr. Zakowsky. The problem was that Mr. Zakowsky's apartment looked out over the enclosed area behind their building. Although it was heavily overgrown with weeds, and the shrubs grew wild, Mr. Zakowsky cherished his view of this so-called garden. It was also the only unpaved area where Anthony could take Zorbo for a walk. Although Anthony religiously cleaned up after Zorbo, Mr. Zakowsky continued to complain bitterly about the dog.

Anthony arrived at his school without further incident. After checking at the office, he found his way to his homeroom. He was early, and the classroom was still empty. He had no idea where he was supposed to sit and was still standing awkwardly in front of the room when the teacher came in. Miss Buenoventi greeted him with a big smile.

"You must be Anthony, my new student."

"Yes ma'am," was his shy answer.

"Anthony, we are happy to have you here in our school. I understand that the school you attended last year was much smaller, and this big building must be a little confusing to you."

"Yes ma'am," was once again the quiet answer.

"Well, I find it very clever of you to have found this classroom all by yourself and gotten here so early. Since you are early, take a good seat. Why don't you take the desk right here in front?"

Anthony had barely selected a seat and sat down when the rest of the students literally stormed in. The noise from their chatter was not at all like the quiet decorum Anthony was used to in his previous school.

Most of his new classmates seemed to know each other. Anthony was grateful that no one paid much attention to him. The run-in with the bullies on his way to school was still very much on his mind, and he was fearful of any new confrontation. He felt ill at ease. It didn't help that the other kids seemed to ignore some of Miss Buenoventi's instructions. He was not used to the way kids talked back to her. During lunch he sat by himself in the cafeteria and silently ate his sandwich. He returned to his classroom long before the lunch period had ended. In the classroom he found Miss Buenoventi, who was eating her lunch at her desk. She seemed happy to see him.

"Well, Anthony, how do you like it so far?"

"It seems pretty nice, Miss Buenoventi."

"Anthony, I have checked a little more on your background. You have come to us from a pretty nice school in a very good neighborhood. The kids in this school are rougher than what you are used to. When they give you any trouble, you come to me, okay?"

"Yes ma'am."

"Promise?" Anthony looked at Miss Buenoventi and nodded his head yes. She was smiling at him, and he wondered why she was teaching at this school when she knew the kids were so unruly. He could not understand why the students seemed to have so little respect for this nice lady.

As the end of the school day approached, Anthony became more and more fearful of the walk home. By the time he was ready to leave the building, his heart was pounding. As he stepped outside the school gate, Zorbo came running up to him, furiously wagging his tail.

"Is that your dog?" the homeless man sitting on the bench at the nearby bus stop asked.

"Yes sir, he is." The smile on Anthony's face told of the relief he felt now that he had his best friend with him for the walk home. As Anthony bent down to give Zorbo a big hug, the man added, "He's been here all damn day. Even refused to leave when some kids tried to chase him away."

III

Previously Anthony had attended Crosswood Academy, a prestigious private school. Academically, he was ahead of the rest of the kids in his new class. But as at the academy, he was again the youngest in his class. He had difficulty making friends, and it did not help that he was conscious of being short and pudgy. Yuni kept telling him not to worry about his height. His father, who was six foot four, had not started growing till he was in junior high, when he suddenly shot up. Anthony tried to believe he would grow up to resemble his father, but the reality was that right now, he was the youngest and shortest kid in the class and often the butt of cruel jokes.

"Hey, teacher's pet, come over here. We have something to show you." Recess was just ending, and everyone was piling back into the classroom. Miss Buenoventi was out for the day, and the substitute had not arrived yet. Tony, one of the boys who was always picking on Anthony, was standing in the back of the classroom and signaled Anthony to come over. Anthony suspected trouble, but he knew the whole class would start needling him if he refused to go over and see what Tony was holding. As he approached the back of the classroom, Tony threw something at him. Anthony quickly put his hands up so the object would not hit him in the face. The object hit his hand and fell to the floor.

The class was howling with laughter, and when Anthony looked down to see what hit him, he saw it was a mouse. The fall must have knocked the creature unconscious because it just lay there and did not try to get away. Anthony bent down and carefully picked up the mouse. He cradled the creature in his hand and started to carry it out the door. The girls were shrieking with laughter, and the boys were chanting, "Anthony has a mouse, a mouse for a mouse." On his way out the door, Anthony bumped into the substitute teacher.

"And what the hell do you think you're doing?"

"I'm going to put this mouse outside, sir."

"Do you think it's funny upsetting the class by bringing a mouse into the building? Is that your joke for the substitute teacher?"

"I did not bring the mouse into the classroom, sir."

"Yes he did," Tony yelled. A few of the other boys and even several girls quickly chimed in. "Yes he did, and he's lying!"

"What's your name?"

"Anthony, sir."

"Well, Anthony, you go put that mouse outside and then march yourself to the principal's office. I'll call and let him know you're coming. Now get out of my sight! As for the rest of you, I have news for you. You are not going to have fun with this substitute teacher. Just calm down and take your seats. All of you be quiet, or I'll keep the entire class after school!"

Anthony knocked softly on the principal's door. His knees were literally shaking when he was told to enter. The fat man with the heavy horn-rimmed glasses stared at him without saying anything. He just sat behind his desk and looked at Anthony. Finally he spoke.

"So you are Anthony. Miss Buenoventi always tells me what a fine young man you are. Looks like you have her fooled. Making fun of a substitute teacher is not considered acceptable in my school. Do you understand that?"

"I did not make fun of the teacher, sir."

"Oh, so you believe that bringing a mouse into the classroom and upsetting the entire class is acceptable behavior, do you?"

"Sir, I really did not bring the mouse into the classroom."

"And Mr. Wilkerson, the substitute teacher, did not catch you with the mouse in your hand?"

"The mouse was thrown at me, sir. I could feel that it was still alive, and I was trying to put it outside."

"Thrown at you? And who threw it at you?" Anthony stood head down, silently looking at his shoes. He knew if he said it was Tony, the next time

Tony and his friends caught him alone, they would beat him. He would rather just not say anything than get beat-up again. He was still sore from the last time they repeatedly punched him in the stomach for having done his homework when the rest of the class had tried to get out of it by denying that Miss Buenoventi had ever assigned it.

"Well, speak up. Who threw it?" Anthony continued his silence. "So you're lying. You did do it!" Again Anthony said nothing. "If you can't admit to the truth, I have a good remedy for that. At the same time, it will teach you not to try to disrupt the class when you have a substitute teacher. You are suspended for three days. You will go to the office to pick up a letter stating that you have been suspended due to misbehavior. You will be allowed to resume classes after three days, only after you have handed in this letter signed by both your parents. Is that clear?"

"I only have a mother, sir."

"Don't try to be cute by correcting me. The office will know about your personal circumstances. Now go on. The letter should be ready in a few minutes."

As usual Zorbo was waiting outside, but as if sensing something was wrong, the dog did not jump all over Anthony when he saw him come out of school. Slowly, the two of them made their way home. Not knowing how to explain his suspension to Yuni, Anthony considered not saying anything about being suspended from school. But he had never lied to his mother. He decided to explain to her that he had been the victim of a joke gone totally wrong. He would stress that he had not been the instigator and certainly had not brought the mouse into the classroom. He would tell her that the substitute teacher had misunderstood what was going on and had totally overreacted. Without stretching the truth, this is what had actually happened.

He didn't want to tell her about Tony and what he had done. That way he would not have to worry her about all the teasing and the many times he had been beaten up by Tony and his friends. He knew Yuni was depressed about the turn their lives had taken and that she fretted continually because she could not provide a better life for him. Her only joy was his academic success. He knew he had to pretend that he loved his new school and didn't miss his friends at Crosswood Academy.

When Anthony arrived home early and starting explaining about the failed joke and his three-day suspension, Yuni wasn't buying. "Anthony, don't treat your mother like an imbecile! Nobody gets suspended for three days for a bad joke they did not initiate. Now tell your mother what really happened."

"Mom, it's true. Some of the boys pulled a joke on me, and the substitute teacher went berserk. He was sure we tried to upset things just to make his life difficult."

"Fine, and who are these so-called friends, and where did this mouse come from?"

"Come on, Mom, it was a bad joke, nothing more."

"Anthony, stop it! I might have lost my leg, but there is nothing wrong with my brain! Now tell me the truth, what happened?" Yuni rarely mentioned the loss of her leg. Because she did so now, Anthony realized she was afraid he might have lost some of his respect for her because of her handicap.

"You're angry because I got suspended."

"I'm not angry, I want the truth. Stop lying to your mother. I don't believe a word of that stupid story of yours!"

Anthony burst out in tears. "Mom, I'm sorry. I did not mean to lie to you. I love you. I don't want you to have to worry about me." Yuni reached out to him.

"Come here and tell your mother what happened." Anthony rushed over to Yuni and buried his head in her lap with such force that he pushed her wheelchair back several inches.

"Mom, I really did not mean to hurt you. I try so hard to make you proud of me, and now I messed everything up." Yuni cradled Anthony's head and gently rubbed her fingers through his hair. When he calmed down a little, she lifted his head and wiped away his tears.

"You're the best son anyone ever had, and I am very proud of you. I understand that you are trying to protect me and keep me from worrying, and I love you. You are my hero. We'll get through this together; we always have. Now calmly tell me exactly what happened."

After Anthony had told her about how Tony had thrown the mouse at him and that he was on his way to put the poor thing outside when the substitute teacher arrived, Yuni decided to go to the school to straighten things out with the principal.

"Mom, please don't do that. I'll never be able to go back again; Tony and his friends will get even with me. Please, Mom, don't do it."

"Anthony, we can't just let them get away with this. If your father were still alive, this never would have happened. I got you into this situation, and I won't let them treat you this way. I'll go speak to your teacher, Miss Buenoventi. I'm sure she'll protect you from those bastards."

"Please, I beg you, Mom, don't go to school. Let me handle it my way. If you go to the principal or Miss Buenoventi, I'll never be able to go back."

"We can't just accept this and let it pass by as if nothing happened. Go get Aunt Rita. She'll know what to do."

"Why Aunt Rita? She won't know about this type of thing. She doesn't even have any children of her own."

"She's lived in this neighborhood much longer than we. She knows these people, and she is smart. She'll know how to handle this. I trust her judgment."

"Mom, let me handle this. I'll just go back to school in three days, and the whole thing will have blown over."

"Anthony, don't argue. Go get Aunt Rita." Reluctantly Anthony left to get her.

Rita, the next-door neighbor, and Yuni had become very close friends. Like Yuni, Rita felt like she did not belong in the neighborhood. The two women also shared the fact that each had enjoyed a brief but highly successful modeling career. After giving up modeling, Rita had started her own beauty salon in an upscale neighborhood. The venture was an immediate success and provided Rita with a comfortable living, surrounded by her well-to-do friends and courted by many influential men, either married or unwilling-to-commit singles.

Life was good for Rita, until the trophy wife of a US senator got badly burned by the hair-coloring chemicals used in Rita's salon. The burns left some very nasty scars that could not be completely removed by plastic surgery, and her scalp was so badly burned that she never regained all of her hair. The civil suits bankrupted the salon. Since Rita could not escape personal liability, she even lost all her personal assets. In time she might have been able to recover financially had it not been for the fact that the senator used his political influence to help bring criminal charges against her.

It turned out that Rita was never licensed to operate a beauty salon. She had used her position as a famous model to get the city and state permits, but she had never finished the courses required to get her certificates. The district attorney also brought charges based on the fact that the coloring chemicals used in her salon were not approved for general use and had been known to cause serious burns when used on people with exceptionally light skin. Rather than face a trial, Rita accepted a plea, which put her in jail for six months and placed her on five years probation. When she was released from jail, her friends quickly distanced themselves from her. Her gentleman friends avoided her like the plague. She tried to find a job, but the best she could do was a job in a small nail salon on 125th Street. Despite her meager income, she barely qualified for an apartment in the same building where Yuni and Anthony now lived.

Rita carefully listened to Anthony's account of what happened. "And what else has been going on between Tony and you?" Yuni had a questioning expression on her face.

"Why do you ask that, Rita?"

"Things like this never happen all by themselves. They are always part of a situation that has been building for quite a while. Anthony is the new kid. He is on their territory. Now, they are testing him." When Anthony didn't answer right away, Rita walked over to him and pulled up his shirt. Yuni let out a gasp. The entire left side of Anthony's chest, lower abdomen, and part of his back was black and blue. "Just about a mouse, is that right, young fellow?"

"Leave me alone, it's not your business." Anthony ran into Yuni's bedroom. Yuni wheeled her chair around and tried to follow.

"Hold on, Yuni, let him go," Rita said. "He needs a moment by himself. When boys get beat-up, they feel ashamed, even if they were vastly outnumbered."

"But my baby, he's hurt. I have to go to him."

"No, just leave him be for a few minutes. I assure you he's okay."

"Why didn't I notice? He's all black and blue."

"You didn't notice because he didn't want you to notice. Obviously, he doesn't want to worry you. In his own way, he's protecting you from the realities of this neighborhood."

"We must go to the school and complain to the principal. He has to know what has been going on, and he has to put a stop to it. Will you go with me?"

"No, and you're not going either. Look, Anthony's pride has been hurt a lot more than his body. Those few black and blue marks will go away all by themselves, but we have to give him a chance to win back his pride."

"Rita, you're talking crazy. The school has to protect him, or I'm taking him out of that school."

"Oh, that's a great solution! What school would you send him to? And he'll feel even worse than he does now."

"So what is your suggestion?"

"Send him back to school in three days and let him solve this in his own way. I have watched that kid of yours. He is tough, and he is smart enough to know he has to solve this without adult assistance."

"You're suggesting I send him back by himself, so he can be beaten up again by those lousy bastards? You've got to be kidding!"

"He's not going to get beat-up."

"How can you be so sure?"

"Yuni, no offense, but you are still living in another world. I have lived here longer than you; I understand the mentality here because I also work in a rough neighborhood. I had to win the respect of my peers, and it wasn't always easy. Even after my colleagues in the shop accepted me, our customers tried to avoid being helped by me for the longest time."

Anthony came back into the living room and sat down close to his mother. "I'm sorry, Mom, I should have told you. But I didn't want to make you unhappy. I know you don't like it here, but you really don't have to worry about me. I'll be okay. Those kids are not going to drive me away. They can make fun of me, but I get much better grades than they do. I'm smarter than they are. They don't have a mom who helps them with their homework and tells them that if they work hard and stay out of trouble, someday they'll move back to Central Park. Don't worry, Mom. I know you're right. I'll work hard and get us out of here, I promise."

"Anthony, come over here. I need to give you a big hug." Anthony could feel Yuni's tears as she pressed his face against her cheek.

Rita stood up. She thought it was a good time to leave mother and son alone, but then she abruptly changed her mind. "Anthony, I'm not working tomorrow. So, if your mother doesn't mind, I would like to take you up to the place where I work and show you off to the girls I work with. If you hang around here all day, people will ask why you're not in school, and it's none of their business." Yuni looked a little hurt, and Rita quickly added, "Yuni, if you feel up to it, you are welcome to join us. It'll be fun; the three of us can have lunch someplace and spend the whole day together."

Rita was right; the three of them did have a lot of fun that day. Rita had an extra surprise for Anthony. Next to the nail salon where she worked was a leather boutique where they sold the type of leather jacket many of the boys, and even some of the girls, in his school wore.

"Let's see if they have your size," Rita said after she had urged Anthony to take a look at the jackets on display in the window.

"No, Rita, we can't afford that."

"Don't worry, Yuni, this will be my treat. Remember, I am borrowing Anthony for the day. He's my boy for the day. First I got the girls in the nail salon jealous, and now I want to buy him a jacket. Come on, Yuni, let me have some fun." Anthony was so excited that he was getting a real leather jacket, just like the other kids wore; there was no way Yuni could refuse to let Rita buy it for him.

IV

After three days Anthony went back to school. He dropped off the signed letter at the office and went to his homeroom, where he had to face Miss Buenoventi.

"Hello, Miss Buenoventi, I'm back from my suspension."

"Yes, I can see that, Anthony. Needless to say, I am very disappointed in your behavior."

"I'm really sorry for what happened, ma'am. It was a bad joke, and it really got a little out of hand. I didn't mean to upset Mr. Wilkerson." Miss Buenoventi was not convinced.

"And mice just come flying out of nowhere in this classroom. Funny I never saw them!" Anthony said nothing. "Well, it was your choice to take the blame. I guess the punishment was appropriate. We won't discuss it any further. Go ahead and sit down."

"Thank you, ma'am."

Anthony was surprised that a couple of the kids said hello to him as they came past his desk on the way to their seats. One of the girls even smiled at him as she passed and said, "Welcome back, we missed you."

The biggest surprise came at recess when Tony came up to him. Anthony fully expected another unpleasant confrontation. He thought Tony was once again making fun of him when he said, "Hey, man, I want to thank you." Then he realized Tony was serious. "It would have been my third suspension, and that means out for good. My old man would have killed me. Thanks again. I owe you one."

With that, Tony walked away to join his friends. It wasn't till the next day that Anthony fully realized that Tony had come over to tell him that the harassing was over and that he was now accepted as part of the class. When Anthony told Yuni about this big change in school, she confessed that she had prayed all day for his safety on the first day he returned to school. She insisted that he run over to Rita's apartment to tell her the news.

A couple of weeks later, Anthony's new status among his classmates was put to the test. School was letting out for the day, and as Anthony came out the main door, he saw several kids throwing stones at Zorbo, who was waiting for him in the usual spot. Anthony ran to Zorbo, yelling, "Leave my dog alone."

"What are you going to do about it?" one of the kids yelled back."

"Leave my dog alone, I said." Anthony kept running toward Zorbo. The group turned from Zorbo and started throwing things at Anthony.

"Cut that out!" someone yelled.

"Says who?" was the reply from the group of stone throwers.

"I said so, now cut it out."

"You gonna make us?"

"Yes," Tony said as he stepped forward. "If you don't stop, I'll knock your fucking head off."

"You and who else?"

"Okay, guys, let's knock the shit out of this bunch of assholes." With that, about eight of Tony's friends jumped on the group that had been bothering Anthony and literally did what Tony had promised.

Unfortunately, Anthony's new status as part of the group and the protection that came with it did not reach much beyond the school grounds. Anthony experienced this the hard way. Yuni had signed him up for swimming lessons at the local YMCA. He had objected strenuously, but Yuni insisted he needed the exercise. Anthony's strong objections stemmed from the fact that his chubby physique gave him rather pronounced breasts. He was afraid to take off his shirt out of fear that kids would laugh at his large nipples. He solved this problem by telling the swimming instructor that he had been badly burned and had large scars on his back. The instructor readily agreed to let him keep his shirt on.

This little white lie worked well for Anthony until the day two boys from the basketball team caught him in the dressing room. As he always did, Anthony had waited till all the other kids from the swim class had finished dressing before he entered the locker

"Sure, I got into Alice's ass."

"You butt-fucked fat Alice?"

Tim loosened his belt and let his pants drop to the floor, "Yes, and now I'm going to get this little bugger."

"Alice is big and fat, but at least she's a girl. This is a boy!"

"He's got tits, doesn't he, so what's the difference?" Anthony tried to wiggle loose, but Victor had him in an iron grip. He prayed someone would come into the locker room to rescue him. He felt Tim's hand guiding his penis in between his cheeks. His throat and mouth ached from the sour bile coming up from his stomach.

When Tim pushed his penis between his cheeks, something in Anthony's brain snapped. Suddenly the fear was gone, and he was filled with rage. Adrenaline rushed through his body; he could feel the strength surge back into his legs. As if he exploded, he bounced up, throwing Tim backward to the floor. Victor lost his grip on him and awkwardly stood facing him. Anthony's right arm swung to the rear, and when it came back, it propelled his fist straight into Victor's nose; he heard a loud crack, and Victor's face was covered with blood. Anthony pulled up his trunks and turned to face Ted. Ted scrambled to his feet and reached down to pull up his pants. Before he got them up to his knees, Anthony's foot came crashing into his crotch. Ted let out a piercing yell and fell to the floor, both hands clasping his genitals.

Mr. Alpers, the swimming instructor, heard Ted's loud yell. He burst into the locker room. "Victor, what happened?" Victor tried to wipe the blood from his face.

"Nothing, sir."

"Anthony, tell me what happened here. Why is Ted in such pain?" Anthony did not answer, but he looked straight at Mr. Alpers, who was surprised to see the defiant look on his face. "Okay, don't tell me, but from the looks of things, you took care of matters real well. Victor, go splash some cold water on your face, and Ted, you get up off the floor and stop crying like a baby. Looks like the two of you got what you deserve! I want you to hand in your YMCA passes, and I don't want to see either of you two around here for at least a month. Anthony, follow me to my office."

In his office Mr. Alpers tried to question Anthony once more about what had happened. "Anthony, unless you explain what happened, I can't do anything more. I have a faint suspicion what those two were up to, and I think I have to call the police to report them. But I can't do a thing unless you explain things to me."

"It was just a fight, and I beat them up."

"Yeah, so I noticed. I might add you did a pretty good job of it. But without you telling me what happened, those two will get away with whatever they were planning." Anthony remained silent. "Okay, have it your way. Now get out of here, tiger."

When Anthony returned home, Yuni noticed a certain confident swagger he had not exhibited before. "Anthony, what's wrong with your foot? Why are you limping?"

"I think I broke my toe when I stubbed it in the locker room at the YMCA."

"Come here, and let me take a look at it. Anthony, your hand is all swollen too! What really happened? Have you been fighting?"

"I guess so, but I didn't start it! Some kids called me fat, and I didn't like it."

V

"For the last couple of years, I have been watching you practice your swimming, and I have discussed with Mr. Alpers the possibility of you joining our YMCA wrestling team." Anthony got excited.

"Really, Mr. Fritz? Do you think I can make the team?" To be asked to be on the wrestling team was quite an honor. Mr. Fritz's teams had won the overall city championship three years in a row and had captured no less than four individual state titles.

"Mr. Alpers tells me you are quite strong for your age, and I'm impressed with your training discipline. You seem determined to improve yourself. That's the type of young man I want on my team. You're a little short and a bit too heavy, but I'm sure that will change in the coming year. You'll do fine on our practice squad. What do you say? Would you like to join up?"

Anthony could hardly believe his good luck. He had never dreamt he would be asked to join the wrestling team. Every boy in the YMCA wanted to be on Mr. Fritz's wrestling team. But they all knew it was very hard to qualify, and Mr. Fritz hardly ever accepted anyone without a rigorous tryout.

"Of course, Mr. Fritz, I would love to join the team." Anthony hesitated. "Would I have to quit my swimming lessons?"

"No, on the contrary. I would urge you to continue. Swimming is good exercise, and it will help you develop your body. Mr. Alpers does not have enough candidates to put together a competition team, and he feels it would be good for you to join us."

Anthony rushed home to tell Yuni the good news, but she was not at all happy that he would join the wrestling team. "Anthony, that is a terrible sport! You know I can't stand to watch it, and you'll get hurt when the bigger boys throw you around and pounce on you."

"Mom, this is scholastic wrestling. It's close to what you have seen in the Olympics. It's not at all like that stuff they show on television."

"Are you sure they won't throw you around and punch you in the face?"

Anthony could not help but laugh. "No, Mom, this is a real sport. You have to come to a match. You'll see it's not at all like what you think. Of course, I won't be able to compete this year, but if I practice hard, Coach Fritz might give me a chance next year."

Having been selected for the wrestling team gave Anthony a tremendous boost of self-confidence. But soon he had to learn that he could not handle every situation all by himself. He had taken Zorbo down to the enclosed area behind their building and was waiting for the dog to do his business somewhere in the overgrown area when three teenage boys approached him.

"Hey, fella, that's a nice leather jacket you're wearing." Anthony did not recognize the boys and did not expect any trouble.

"Yes, it's nice, got it as a present."

"It's so nice, I think I want to have it. I think I will take it from this kid." One of the boys reached for Anthony, and the other two egged him on.

"Take it from the little fart; he don't need a nice jacket like that." Anthony pushed the boy's arm back and stood facing him with both fists balled, ready to land a punch if the boy dared put out his arm again.

"Get the hell away from me. I won't give you my jacket, and I'll beat the hell out of you if you dare touch me." This response caused great hilarity among the three. Rather than back off, they jumped on Anthony. Anthony started swinging wildly at his attackers but could not land a punch. When the three of them grabbed him, he struggled with all his might but could not hold them off.

"Give us the damn jacket, or you'll really get hurt."

"Fuck you. You ain't getting it."

"This will persuade you!" One of the boys pulled out a knife and held it to Anthony's throat while the other two pinned his arms down.

"Zorbo, Zorbo, come help," Anthony yelled.

"Shut up! Yell once more, and I'll kill you!" Anthony could feel the point of the blade push against his throat. Just before it could break his skin, Zorbo came flying toward them. The dog leaped up and bit down hard on the hand holding the knife. The force with which Zorbo came flying in threw the attacker to the ground. Zorbo was all over him. Snarling, with foam coming from his mouth, Zorbo bit into the boy's stomach, tearing his clothes and drawing blood. Anthony was relieved Zorbo had stopped the attack on him with the knife, but at the same time, he was afraid Zorbo might actually kill the kid.

"Zorbo, let go! Come here, now!" Zorbo let go immediately. As soon as the dog let go, the boy got up and ran away as fast as he could, closely followed by his two companions. Still shaken from the attack, Anthony knelt next to Zorbo. "Good dog. Zorbo is the best dog. Quick, let's go upstairs before they decide to come back with more of their friends."

Later that night there was a knock on their door. "Anthony, go see who that is. It's late; don't let them in without checking with me."

"It's the police with some other man."

"Okay, hold on, I'm coming." When Yuni wheeled up to the front door, Anthony opened the door to let the police officers in.

"Sorry to disturb you, madam. I'm Officer Murphy, and this is Sergeant Alvarez. We have Mr. Gomez with us from the city dog pound. We are looking for the dog who attacked some kids in the back of this building. Some of your neighbors tell us the dog may belong to you. Do you have a dog?"

"As you can see, we have a dog. He is standing right next to me. But he does not attack anybody. Look, he is quite calm. He likes people."

"Yes, madam, but we have a report that a teenage boy was seriously attacked by a dog in the enclosed area behind your building. Several people saw your son and the dog leave the area earlier this evening."

"Anthony, did you let Zorbo out in the area behind the building?" It looked like Anthony was going to cry.

"Yes, but three kids attacked me and tried to steal the jacket Aunt Rita gave me. Zorbo chased them away." Sergeant Alvarez moved toward the area where Anthony was standing.

"Look, son, your dog might have chased some boys, but what we have to know is, did he bite one of them?"

"They attacked me and tried to steal my coat. They tried to kill me, and Zorbo chased them."

"Now, now, tried to kill you? I guess you got into a fight with those boys. That happens, but did the dog bite one of them?"

"I tell you they tried to kill me. They had a knife. Zorbo protected me."

"Son, we can guess you love that dog, but you must tell us, did he bite that boy?" Anthony did not reply. "Madam, we have a report that this dog bit one of the boys. Mr. Gomez here has to take the dog to the city dog pound."

"You heard my boy. He says they tried to kill him, and the dog protected him, so go arrest those boys that attacked my boy."

"Yes, madam, we understand that your son is trying to protect the dog, but Mr. Gomez must take him away." Anthony placed himself before Zorbo.

"You're not taking him anywhere," he said defiantly.

"My boy does not lie. They attacked him, and the dog only protected him by chasing them away."

"Please, madam, don't make this difficult. We have to take the dog, and we really don't want to bring charges against you for stopping us from doing our duty."

"You're not taking my dog!"

"Please, son, calm down. Mr. Gomez will take good care of him; he's trained to protect dogs from harm."

"If you take my dog, you'll have to take me too. I'm the one who hurt those guys, and they deserved it."

"Son, I promise Mr. Gomez will take good care of your dog. You and your mom can come to the pound in the morning, and the people in charge there will discuss the whole matter with you."

Yuni realized it would be difficult to prevent them from taking Zorbo with them, but she too wanted to protect the dog. "How do you expect us to get to the pound? I'm in a wheelchair, and Anthony here has to go to school. The whole thing is unnecessary. Zorbo is a good dog, and if those hoodlums attacked Anthony, of course the dog would react. That's what dogs do."

Officer Murphy, a big three-hundred-plus gentle giant, could not see himself arresting a woman in a wheelchair and her son for the sole reason that they were protecting their dog. "Madam, we really don't want to cause you and your son any grief, but we have our orders. May I suggest that I come here in the morning to take you and your son in my squad car to the dog pound? In the meantime Mr. Gomez will take good care of Zorbo."

"What about Anthony's school?"

"I'm sure we can take care of that too. Missing one day won't hurt him." Reluctantly Anthony gave in, but not until after Mr. Gomez sat down with him and explained that he would personally see to it that no one mistreated Zorbo and that nothing would happen to the dog until there could be a full hearing as to what happened. Anthony insisted that he be the one to bring Zorbo down to Mr. Gomez's truck and safely put him in the dog cage.

As promised, Officer Murphy arrived early the next morning to take Yuni and Anthony to the dog pound. On arrival at the pound, Anthony was pleased to find Mr. Gomez playing in a dog run with Zorbo. When Zorbo saw Anthony, he ran over, wagging his tail so hard that Anthony had to hold up his hand to prevent getting hit in the face by the wildly swinging tail. While Anthony and Mr. Gomez stayed outside with Zorbo, Yuni and Officer Murphy went inside to meet with the director. The news was not good. As the director explained the situation, the future for Zorbo looked very dim.

"The report from the hospital where the young man was brought for treatment describes a deep bite in his right hand, breaking two bones, several superficial face wounds, and a severe stomach wound that required seven stitches to close. Zorbo will be tested for rabies, and normally, because of the severity of the attack, the law requires that the dog be put down immediately after the test. However, because of the report filed by Officer Murphy, which stated there was conflicting evidence as why the attack took place, and the determination by Mr. Gomez that Zorbo is not a vicious dog, I have prepared a petition for you to request a court hearing to determine if the dog should be put down."

"You mean they would kill Zorbo for protecting Anthony?" Yuni's hands were trembling as she thought about how she would explain this to Anthony.

"Yes, normally I would not have a choice; I would have to put the dog down immediately after the rabies test. You're very lucky Officer Murphy intervened in your behalf. He stated in his report that the owner of the dog strongly disputes the story given to him by the young man who was bitten. If you sign the petition I prepared for you, there will be a hearing to determine what should happen to the dog. I suspect you will get a notice to appear in court about a week from now to tell your side of the story. In the meantime Zorbo has to remain here in the pound. Don't worry, Mr. Gomez will take good care of him. He really likes your dog."

More than a week passed before Yuni received a notice that the court hearing was scheduled for the coming Monday afternoon. During that time Anthony had become obstinate and unruly. He kept obsessing as to what was going to happen to Zorbo. He worried about Zorbo's condition at the dog pound. Was the dog unhappy being locked up there? Did he get enough food?

He got so depressed about what was happening to Zorbo that he said to Yuni, "It's all my fault. I should not have called Zorbo to come and help me. I should have just given them the damn coat, and none of this would have happened."

"Don't talk crazy," was her response. "They were looking for a fight more than for your coat. Either way, they would have hurt you." Anthony's sulking about his dog led him to skip swimming lessons, and he even failed to show up for wrestling practice. If Yuni had not been aware of this and had not called Mr. Fritz to explain the situation, he could have been thrown off the team. What Yuni did not know was that Anthony had stopped going to school. Instead, he just hung around the street all day.

Finally, the day of the hearing arrived. Yuni asked Rita to come along for support. The three of them arrived at the courthouse several hours before their case was scheduled to be heard. By the time it was their turn, the courtroom had pretty much emptied out. Yuni glanced around the empty room, and to her horror noticed Mr. Zakowsky sitting in the next to last row.

She quickly turned to Rita and whispered, "Oh my God, look who's here. It's that horrible Zakowsky man. Now we're really in trouble. He'll say all kinds of bad things about us having Zorbo in the building."

"Just ignore him," Rita told her. "Whatever he has to say has no bearing on what happened when Zorbo bit that boy. The judge won't even let him talk. Calm down, the bailiff is about to call us."

They had agreed that Yuni would do all the talking and that Anthony would only speak if the judge directed a question directly at him. Not until she was called and had wheeled herself in front of the judge did Yuni realize that the well-dressed young man sitting in the front row was the boy who had attacked Anthony.

The judge turned to Yuni and asked, "Are you Mrs. Yuni Abayari, the mother of Anthony Walker?"

"Yes, Your Honor."

"And where is Anthony?"

"He is here, Your Honor. I told him to stay seated unless you called for him."

"Well, I want him up here. Anthony, come stand here next to your mother." The judge turned to the well-dressed kid sitting in the front row. "And you are Anthony Hines?"

"Yes, Your Honor."

"Step up here in front of me. Did you bring anyone with you?"

"Yes, Your Honor, my father, James Hines."

"Step up here, Mr. Hines, and stand next to your son. So we have two Anthonys with separate stories as to what happened on the night that you, Anthony Hines, claim to have been attacked by Anthony Walker's dog."

"Okay, Anthony Hines, tell us what you claim happened."

"Me and two friends were taking a shortcut through a little park right behind Anthony's house when he was standing there. I think he was waiting for his dog. When we passed him, we started funning with him, and one of my buddies called him fatso. He got mad and started hitting at us. We pushed back, and he called for his dog. That's when the dog attacked me and bit me."

"You're lying. That's not what happened." The judge quietly admonished Anthony for his outburst.

"You'll get a chance to speak, but do not interrupt when I am talking to someone else."

"Say you're sorry," Yuni hissed at him.

"I'm sorry, Your Honor, but it did not happen that way."

"Okay, then tell us what you claim happened."

"I was walking my dog in the usual place behind our building when three guys I did not know attacked me. They wanted my coat. When I didn't give it to them, they came after me. While the two other guys held me, Anthony here held a knife to my throat and demanded I give him my coat. That's when I called my dog, who came running to protect me."

"Oh, I see. Anthony had a knife and demanded your coat. Mr. Hines, can you tell me how many coats your son has?"

"I don't know for sure, Your Honor, but I would say at least four."

This time it was Yuni who spoke out of turn. "How many coats he has does not mean a thing. Those boys were looking for a fight, and when my boy says they attacked him, that is true. My boy does not lie, and his dog is a good dog. Anthony takes good care of him, and he was protecting his master."

"Mrs. Abayari, of course you believe what your son tells you, and I understand that he is trying to save his dog. But from the wounds reported by the hospital, I have to conclude that this was a very serious attack by your son's dog, and there is no evidence your son was threatened by a knife. It appears to me that this is a rather dangerous dog."

"He's not dangerous, Your Honor. We've had him for many years, and there never has been any trouble."

"You had him for many years, but according to the records before me, you never bothered to have a vet give him his rabies shots. You haven't even bought his dog tags."

"We don't have money for such things, Your Honor."

"I can appreciate that, but I can't allow you to expose other people to this dangerous animal who was not even protected against rabies. I'm very sorry, but we have to put the animal down."

The judge had hardly finished his sentence, when someone shouted from the back of the room, "You kan't kill dat dog!"

"If you're not quiet, I'll have you removed from my courtroom," the judge shouted back.

"I sad dat you kan't kill dat dog. I know whot happened."

"Who are you, and how would you know what happened?"

"I am John Zakowsky, and I seen whot happened."

"If that is true, I would like for you to come up here and explain to this court what you saw." John Zakowsky moved quickly to the front of the courtroom. He looked at Yuni, who was staring at him in disbelief.

"I lif in de same building as dis lady here. I lif in de back of de building, and my apartment looks down over de little park in de back. I seen de boys come up to Anthony. I kan't hear wot dey saying, but I seen dat boy here put a knife to Anthony's sroat. Dat dog came just in time to rescue Anthony."

The judge looked rather skeptical. "You're not just making that up to help save this dog, are you?"

"I, John Zakowsky, never tell a lie in my lif. Besides, I hate dat dog. He don't belong in our building."

"Then why come forward to save him?"

"I saw whot was happening, but I am too old and slow to rush down and help de boy. If dat boy get hurt or even killed, it is Zakowsky's fault, people say, he is too old and slow to help. Dat dog saved me from dat burden. Dat dog is a hero. John Zakowsky says you kan't kill him!"

"Mr. Zakowsky, you actually saw Anthony Hines hold a knife to Anthony Walker's throat?"

"I said John Zakowsky never makes up stories. Yes sir, I saw dat!" The judge turned to the bailiff.

"I want Anthony Hines turned over to the DA's office so they can further investigate what is an apparent assault with a deadly weapon. Take him out of here."

When the bailiff had removed Anthony Hines and his father, the judge turned to Anthony. "You can thank Mr. Zakowsky, who apparently does not really like your dog, for coming forward and verifying that what you told us is the truth. It seems your dog is guilty of nothing more than protecting his master. That he was a little heavy-handed in doing so can only be explained by his love for you. You can go directly from here to pick up your dog at the pound. Come with me to my office, and I'll sign a release order for you to take with you."

Anthony stood stock-still and stared at the judge, then he bent down and put his head in Yuni's lap. All the pent-up emotions came loose, and he started crying. When Yuni had managed to calm him down, Anthony stood up and went over to Mr. Zakowsky.

To everyone's utter amazement, not the least Mr. Zakowsky's, he gave the old man a huge hug.

"Thank you, thank you. I promise, I'll never say anything bad about you again!"

VI

The story of the attack on Anthony by the three boys trying to steal his coat quickly spread among the kids in his school. What made the story particularly exciting was the way Zorbo had come to his rescue. Zorbo was dubbed "the Wonder Dog," and there was always a group of admirers around him when he sat in his usual spot waiting for Anthony to come out of school. Zorbo was not the only one who had become a celebrity: Anthony himself had also gained in popularity during the school year. He had started to grow, and he had slimmed down quite a bit. He was an exceptionally bright student, but he not only got straight As, he was also always ready to help the other kids in his class with their homework.

One of his classmates who relied on him for help was Princess. Princess was a tall beautiful girl with long black hair and striking hazel eyes. Unfortunately, what she had in physical attributes, she lacked in brainpower. Princess had already failed two grades and would surely fail again if not for all the help she received from Anthony. Anthony spent hours before and after school tutoring Princess. She was especially poor in math, and he had to explain everything in its simplest concept before she had a clue on how to finish her math assignments.

Anthony and Princess were sitting in Miss Buenoventi's classroom, just the two of them. School was over for the day, and Anthony was tutoring Princess for a math test scheduled for the next day. After about the tenth time that Anthony showed her how to solve one of the simpler problems, Princess exclaimed, "I've got it! I really understand it now. Anthony, I am so grateful. You have helped me so much! If I pass this year, it's all because of you. I should get you something. What would you like?"

"That's really not necessary. I was glad to help, and I hope you can be in our class next year."

"But I want to. I have to do something for you."

"Really, you don't have to."

"Would you like to feel me up? All the other boys are always trying."

"Come on, Princess, it's okay like this. I am happy to help you."

"But I want you to. Here, feel my breast." With that she took Anthony's hand and placed it on her breast. Hesitantly Anthony rubbed his hand gently over the front of Princess's blouse. "Not like that, silly. Here, I'll help you." Princess unbuttoned her blouse and pushed Anthony's hand inside her bra. Anthony carefully cupped her breast. "Boy, you are green! Not like that. Use your fingers and run them back and forth across my nipple. You'll feel it get nice and hard."

Anthony quickly withdrew his hand. He could feel his ears burn from embarrassment. "We don't have to do this. I said I was happy to help you."

"Okay, I have a better idea. If I pass the test tomorrow, we go to my house, and I'll let you go all the way." Anthony had been around the other boys long enough to understand what she meant.

"Princess, I just wanted to help you. You don't have to pay me back. Really, you owe me nothing."

"Hey, you don't know what you're passing up. I am offering to do you for free. The super in my building gives me twenty-five dollars each time I let him screw me." Anthony did not like what he heard. He had never thought of Princess in that way. This was new for him. Although he had to admit to himself that he had had a crush on her, and maybe even fantasized about her, he had never thought of her as quite so promiscuous. Going to bed with the super for money really destroyed the sweet girl image he had of her.

"Princess, I don't want to do that. Let's just leave it this way and just be friends."

"What's the matter? You either don't like girls, or you think I'm dirty because I do it with the super."

"Princess, please, let's just prepare for tomorrow's test; I really don't want to do it with you."

"Well, all the other guys are hot to do it with me, and they give me marijuana joints when I let them. You're just a conceited snob. Just because you are smarter than us, you think you're better than us! Well, if you think you're too good to fuck me, I don't need your help either." Princess slammed her books shut and went storming out. Anthony stared after her. His first impulse was to rush after her, but then he realized he would not know what to say to her once he caught up to her.

The next day Princess failed to show up for the math exam. Miss Buenoventi refused to give her a makeup exam and gave her an F. From then on Princess failed almost all of the tests, and once again she failed a grade. Because of her age, she could not repeat the year, and she was forced to leave school.

When school let out for summer vacation, Anthony was old enough to get a summer job. He was lucky and landed a job as towel boy for the YMCA summer camp. This gave him lots of free time to train in the swimming pool, and Coach Fritz showed him how he could start on some light exercises in the weight room to increase his strength for wrestling.

VII

During his junior year in high school, Anthony came into his own. As Yuni predicted, he had shot up and was now well over six feet and still growing. He was not overly muscular, but his body was rock hard, and because of his wide shoulders, he looked well cut. At the beginning of the school year, Coach Fritz had moved him up to the YMCA travel team, and he won several medals in his weight class. During home matches Yuni and Rita could always be found in the bleachers, screaming for joy as he took down his opponent. Rita, especially, went all out. She bought him the sweat suits the team wore during warm-up, and when he came to the sidelines, dripping in sweat after a tough match, she would spend a long time carefully drying him off with the large towels she always brought with her.

Rita's hovering over him embarrassed Anthony, but he never complained about it. The most he would say was, "Aunt Rita, that's enough; it's warm in here, and I won't catch cold." Rita would have none of it.

"No, honey, you are soaking wet. Come here and let me finish drying your back."

Yuni would chime in. "Aunt Rita is right. Let her dry you off before you go back to the bench and join your teammates."

During the regional championships held in Connecticut, Anthony won gold in his weight class. This qualified him to compete in the nationals, which were to be held the next month in Denver. He could hardly wait to get home and tell Yuni. As soon as the bus dropped the team off at the YMCA, he hurried home.

"Mom, I won gold. I'm going to the nationals." Yuni did not answer, and he went racing through the apartment looking for her. He did not even stop to pet Zorbo, who was jumping all over him. He found her in her bedroom, curled up, writhing with pain.

"Mom, what's the matter!"

"Anthony, Anthony, it hurts so bad," she whispered. Anthony was shaking.

"Where does it hurt? What happened?"

"My stomach, my side. It hurt before, but never this bad. Oh, Anthony, I'm sorry. I don't want you to have to worry about me, but this time it hurts so bad." Her voice was weak, and Anthony realized he had to call an ambulance or try to take her to the emergency room. "I'll help you get dressed. We have to go to the emergency room. I'll call a taxi right now."

"No, don't," she whispered. "I know what it is; I took some extra pain pills, and they should start working soon."

"No, we're going to see a doctor. What pain-killers are you talking about? Where did you get them?" Yuni did not answer; she just curled up and held on to her stomach, groaning softly. Anthony grabbed the phone and called 911. "My mother is doubled up in pain. Please send an ambulance. No, I don't know what's wrong. She was not in an accident, but her stomach and side hurt very badly. No, I can't get her to the emergency room. Please send an ambulance!" The 911 operator heard the panic in Anthony's voice and quickly noted down the address.

"The ambulance will be there within twenty minutes."

Anthony turned to his mother. "Hold on, the ambulance is on the way. Just a little while longer, and they will take care of your pain. Mom, do you know what is the matter?" Yuni did not answer. She just lay there doubled up in pain.

The ambulance arrived in less than fifteen minutes; the attendants wrapped Yuni in a blanket and lifted her onto a gurney. They wheeled her into the elevator and quickly got her into the ambulance that was waiting below. One of the attendants turned to Anthony.

"Son, you coming along?" Anthony quickly got into the ambulance and sat beside the gurney. He was holding tightly onto Yuni's hand when the attendant put his hand on his shoulder. "Son, you'll have to move over. I have to give your mom a shot of morphine to help her with this pain."

"Do you know what is hurting her so badly?" Anthony asked.

"No, I don't, but the morphine will help. We'll be at the hospital shortly; don't worry. They'll take good care of her. The doctors will know what to do." Anthony was faintly aware that the ambulance was racing through the streets with the sirens going. Fear was taking hold of him, and he was nearing a state of panic. The attendant noticed and handed him two pills with some water. "Here, take these. They will help you calm down. Don't worry, we're almost at the hospital. Trust me, the doctors are great. They'll take good care of your mom. Don't you worry; everything is going to be okay."

The doctor in the emergency room did not take long to decide to have Yuni rushed into the operating room. Anthony was escorted to a waiting room and told to wait until a doctor came to speak to him. The wait seemed to last forever, but finally a doctor, still dressed in his scrubs, came out to talk him.

"Son, did you know your mother has been having chemo and radiation therapy for several weeks?"

Anthony was stunned. "Impossible. I would have known!"

"I have to assume she was keeping it from you to protect you from having to worry about her."

"No, it's not true! I would have known."

"Sit down, son, and let me explain. Your mother is heavily sedated, but she is in the recovery room, and you can go see her after I tell you what is going on. I understand they gave you some calming pills in the ambulance. Would you like some more to calm you down?"

"No, I'm okay." Anthony felt an icy calm come over him. "I would like to see my mother right now, please!"

"I won't hold you back, but she is heavily sedated and quite groggy; you might first want to hear from me what her condition is." Anthony realized he could best help his mother by staying calm and finding out exactly what they meant about her having chemo treatments.

"Yes, I would appreciate it if you tell me exactly what is wrong with my mother; she never told me about any chemo treatments."

"Normally I would not go into too much detail with you, but I am told that you are her only son, and that there is no other family member we could contact."

"That's correct; it's just my mother and me."

"Your mother's condition is quite serious. Before we had a chance to check all her records, we operated and discovered there was little we could do for her."

"What do you mean by there's little you can do for her, and what records did you check?"

"When we operated, we saw that your mother was suffering from an advanced stage of cancer. It has spread throughout her body, and her major organs are affected."

Anthony felt the blood draining from his head; he thought he was going to faint. He understood quite well what the doctor was telling him. His mother was going to die. He held on to the arms of his chair so tightly that his hands hurt, but he was determined to keep his composure. For his mother's sake, he could not let his emotions get control of him. He could not give in. He was all she had, and he had to take care of her.

"I understand what you're telling me, but what records did you find?"

"From our records we can tell that she came into our hospital a while ago complaining of abdominal and back pains. Based on her history with cancer, several biopsies were taken, and the results showed that her cancer had reoccurred. By the time she was examined, the cancer had already spread, and there was little we could do for her. She insisted she had beaten cancer once before, and if we agreed to give her chemotherapy and radiation treatments, she was sure she could once again beat the cancer. Some of our staff thought chemo and radiation would have little or no effect and that it would not be advisable to put her through the treatments. She insisted—actually, she begged—to have our consent to have the treatments. She was not afraid of the treatments. She had been through it once before, and she could handle it. She was sure it would cure her. Her doctor—he's been called and will see her tomorrow—consented and prescribed very heavy chemotherapy."

"How long do we have, Doctor?"

"We can't let her go home. I'll try to keep her here in the hospital as long as I can, but she might be transferred to hospice." Anthony's head sank into his lap, and he could feel the tears welling up. He kept telling himself, *Don't give in, not now. She needs you now more than ever.*

"Can I get you anything?"

"No thank you, Doctor. I would like to go to my mother now."

When Anthony approached her bed, Yuni had her eyes closed, and it looked like she was asleep. He took her hand in his, and she opened her eyes. She squeezed his hand and said, "I feel better now; the pain is much less. Am I in the hospital?"

"Yes, we took you here in the ambulance."

"Yes, I remember the ambulance. Thank you for taking me here. The pain was so bad; I really did not know what to do."

"Mom, you knew you were sick. Why did you not tell me?" For a while Yuni lay still and did not answer. She started sobbing softly, and Anthony had to lean in to hear what she was saying.

"Oh, Anthony, I am so terribly sorry. Things were going so well, and I did not want to worry you. You seemed so happy. After all that time, you finally seemed happy. I did not want to spoil that."

"But, Mom, you knew what you had. I should have known."

"I'm sorry, but I was so sure I would get better. You know I did before." Anthony did not know what to answer. He was angry that he did not know his mother was sick, but he did not want to make her feel guilty. With tears streaming down his face, he started to explain how he felt. Before he could get started, Rita burst into the room.

Rita bent over Yuni's bed. "Yuni, Yuni, I'm so sorry I wasn't there to help you. You poor thing; you must have been in such pain, and no one there to help." She turned to Anthony. "Thank God you came home in time to take her here. How is she doing?"

"It's very serious, Aunt Rita. The doctors say she's got—"

Rita interrupted him. "Yes, I know; will they be able to help her?"

Anthony ran to Rita, and as he threw his arms around her, he sobbed, "Aunt Rita, my mom is dying. Oh my God, she is dying." Rita tried to hold him close and console him, but Anthony abruptly pulled away and went over to Yuni. He buried his head against her chest and sobbed inconsolably. Yuni slowly rubbed her fingers through his hair.

"I tried, Anthony. I did not want to let you down. I tried to make you happy; I thought we would make it, you and I."

"You made me happy, really you did." Anthony sobbed. "You have done everything for me, Oh, Mom, I love you so much!" Anthony kept on sobbing, and Yuni held him.

Rita stood at the head of the bed and silently watched the two of them. When Anthony stopped crying, Yuni spoke gently to him.

"Anthony, listen very carefully. You are going to be okay. You're strong, and you'll make it. You'll grow up to be a fine man just like your father was. You have his blood; you have it in you to be a success. You will do it." Once again Anthony burst out in tears, and Yuni pulled him tightly to her chest. She turned to Rita. "You promised to take care of him."

"I will, Yuni. I promised, and I will."

"You'll explain to Anthony what we arranged?"

"Of course, Yuni, I'll explain everything; it will be exactly the way you wanted it to be."

VIII

Yuni was kept in the hospital for two days. During that time Anthony stayed at her bedside for almost the entire time. He only left briefly when Rita forced him to go home to shower and change clothes. On the third day, Yuni was moved to hospice. Anthony stayed at her side until the end.

After his mother died, Anthony pulled himself together enough to help Rita make the funeral arrangements. When Anthony was having a bad moment, Rita gently pushed him through it.

"Come on; remember you promised your mom to be strong. She would not have wanted you to give up."

Only a few people attended the funeral, but it was more than Anthony had expected. He thought that only Rita and he would be there. But Rita had called his school to notify them that Anthony's mother was critically ill and had been hospitalized. She later called again to inform them that his mother had passed away and that he would be out of school for a little while longer. Anthony was surprised when people started arriving in the small chapel that was part of the hospice. Miss Buenoventi, his grade-school teacher, was the first to arrive. When Anthony saw her come in, he flew into her arms.

"Thank you, thank you so much for coming." Next to arrive were Coach Fritz and the high school principal. The biggest surprise came when Mr. Zakowsky, accompanied by the building super, walked in. When Anthony went over to greet him, Mr. Zakowsky brushed off his thank you.

"Uf course I'm here. Yur mother was a fine lady, too nice fur our building, I liked her. Did Rita tell you I have been taking care of yur stupid dog while yu was at de hospital?"

"Yes, she did; that was so kind of you. Thank you very much."

"Yu know, dat stupid dog of yurs is kinda nice."

After the funeral Rita and Anthony returned to the apartment, where Zorbo greeted them with great joy. Anthony played with him for a while, and as if the dog could understand, Anthony said, "It's good you don't understand what happened. Zorbo, I wish you could have protected her from her illness, the way you have always protected me."

Rita looked over at them. "He will miss her once he realizes she will not be coming home." As the tears shot into Anthony's eyes, she realized she should not have said that. She went to him to give him a hug. "You can cry. It's not a shame to cry, but we have to keep talking about your mother. We can't pretend it did not happen and that we don't miss her very much. You can talk to me about her. That's better than trying to deal with it all by yourself. I told you we will get through this together."

It was not until several days later that Anthony asked Rita about the arrangements Yuni mentioned in the hospital.

"When the cancer came back, your mother told me that a long time ago she had made a will in which she requested I be appointed your guardian in the event she would die before you reached your eighteenth birthday. Even though she really believed she would once again be cured, she gave me a copy of her will and told me where she kept the original. Do you want me to file her will and ask the court to follow your mother's wishes and appoint me your guardian?"

"Where will I live? Would you still let me finish high school?"

"Of course you'll finish school, and I want you to finish college. You will live with me in my apartment. By law we have to give up this apartment, but that doesn't matter. You're not old enough to live alone; we couldn't afford it anyway. You can bring over the sofa bed your mother bought for you and any other piece of furniture you want to keep. I'll gladly make room for it. My stuff is old, and I can get rid of some things."

"Can Zorbo come?" Rita could not help but laugh.

"Of course Zorbo can come. I love that dog, and I hope you'll share him with me."

"Mom was getting monthly payments from Social Security. What will we do for money?"

"Don't worry about money! I have my income, and as soon as the court appoints me your guardian, I can apply for your Social Security benefits. I will also apply for any benefits you might get from the VA as an army orphan. You're sixteen years old, so you should be getting benefits for at least a couple of years."

"Do you really want me to live with you?" Again Rita had to laugh.

"Come here, silly; let me give you a hug. I adore you and that dog of yours; my apartment will be your home for as long as you want, and I want it that way."

Rita had to do a lot of talking and cajoling to get Anthony to go back to school. He had already missed close to two weeks of school, and she was worried. When he finally returned to school, his classmates welcomed him back, and his teachers made it possible for him to make up the exams he had missed. Anthony had no trouble catching up. It was more difficult for Rita to try to persuade Anthony not to skip the National High School Wrestling Championships in Denver. Coach Fritz had accepted the position of gym teacher at Anthony's high school. Now, Anthony had his mentor as his high school coach. Rita called Coach Fritz and asked him to talk to Anthony. Coach Fritz decided that peer pressure would work best. He asked Anthony's teammates to urge Anthony not to let the team down, but to go to Denver and try to win a medal for the team.

Anthony was still undecided when Rita amped up the pressure. "Your mom would have wanted you to go. She was so proud of your wrestling achievements. Just go and win a medal for her."

Anthony did go, and he dedicated each match to his mother. He fought each match like his life depended on it, and Coach Fritz was surprised at the strength he exhibited. He won every one of his matches and came away with gold in his weight class.

IX

During the summer between his junior and senior year in high school, Anthony got a job at a local grocery store. He started out as a bagger at the checkout, but was soon moved to shelving and labeling. Before the summer was over, he was substituting as cashier. Besides his work, Anthony did not go out much, but he did continue to work out at the YMCA.

When school started in September, Anthony was quite the hero. His gold medal in the national championships had been mentioned in *Sports Illustrated* magazine, and everybody in school seemed to know about it. He was quite a hit with the girls; he had grown to be six four. He had the imposing body of his father, and his face was the masculine version of his beautiful mother. Still, he rarely dated or participated in social functions. He kept his after-school job and continued on the wrestling team. He had little time for anything else.

Since he was determined to keep up a straight-A average, his school work took precedence over all else. He knew his mother had wanted him to go to college, and he had his mind set on getting a full scholarship to one of the better universities. When he discussed this with his mentor, Coach Fritz, the coach told him he could certainly get an athletic scholarship. Coach had just read that ten wrestlers from Princeton had qualified for the NCAA Division 1 Wrestling Championships. He promised to call their coach and propose Anthony for a wrestling scholarship.

When Anthony came in late one evening after wrestling practice, Rita was waiting for him at the door. She had tears in her eyes, and Anthony asked what was wrong.

"It's Zorbo. I found him dead in his basket when I came home."

"No, no, you're wrong. He can't be dead." Anthony ran to Zorbo's basket and took the dog into his arms. "Zorbo, Zorbo, wake up! Please wake up, Zorbo."

Rita came over and put her arms around Anthony's shoulders. "It's no use, Anthony. I tried, but he is dead." Anthony put the dog down slowly and sat down crying next to Zorbo's basket, with one hand still stroking the dog's head.

"Why did you have to go, Zorbo? You're such a great dog. Oh God, I did not want you to go. Why now? You weren't sick."

Rita pulled Anthony to his feet and tried to console him. She held him real tight to her breast and whispered softly, "Zorbo was almost fourteen years old. You gave him a good life, but his time had come. Be thankful he did not suffer. He died in his sleep of old age."

"You really think so? You don't think he suffered while we weren't here to help him?"

"I am sure; he was lying peacefully in his basket when I found him. We have to take him to a vet so he can be properly buried."

"Can't he stay just a little while longer? It's very late now. Can't we take him in the morning?"

"I guess the vet will be closed now anyway. We'll wrap him in a blanket and take him tomorrow morning."

At the vet they said Zorbo could be cremated and buried in a doggie cemetery, but that would cost a lot more than if they disposed of him in the usual way. Anthony chose to have Zorbo buried in the dog cemetery, and he insisted that he pay for it out of the money he had saved from his work.

X

Since the day Anthony moved in with her, Rita had made it a habit to kiss him good night before he went to sleep. The day after Zorbo died, she waited until he was in bed. She bent down over his bed, and instead of kissing him on his forehead, she kissed him on the lips. This surprised Anthony, but he dared not pull away for fear of hurting Rita's feelings. The next night it happened again, but this time the kiss lasted much longer, and Anthony did move his head to the side. He wondered why Rita was doing it, but he did not say anything.

The next night he lay in bed wondering if Rita would kiss him like that again. He saw Rita come out of the bathroom, but instead of her pajamas, she was wearing a very sheer negligee. Anthony could clearly see that she was not wearing anything underneath. He held his breath, wondering what Rita would do.

She came over to his bed, bent over him, and said, "Anthony, you do love me, don't you?"

"Of course I do, Aunt Rita. I love you very much, but what are you doing?"

Rita bent down deeper over his bed. Her negligee had opened in the front, and Anthony could see her bare breasts.

"Aunt Rita, this is not right. You're my aunt. We should not be doing this."

"It's all right, darling. I'm not really your aunt, and I love you so very much."

"Aunt Rita, we can't do this!"

"We love each other, and that makes it all right." While she said that, Rita dropped her negligee to the floor and pulled the blanket back. Before Anthony could move, she lay down on top of him and started kissing him.

She held her hands on both sides of his head and looked him straight in the eye.

"Anthony, you know I am not your real aunt. It's okay for us to make love. But if you don't want to, I'll stop right now and go to my room. I'll never force you. I love you too much to do that." Anthony did not say anything for a while. He could feel her body pressing against his, and his body started to react. It did not help that Rita was still a good-looking woman—maybe not quite the beauty she had been in her modeling days. But she had taken great care of her body, and it showed.

Without a word Anthony threw both his arms around Rita's neck and pulled her face against his. He started kissing her wildly, and Rita responded by pushing her tongue between his teeth and opening his mouth. After a while Rita rolled next to him, and she took his hand to let him stroke her breasts. When Anthony kissed her breasts, Rita could feel her nipples harden. Again she reached for his hand, but this time she guided it between her legs.

"Go ahead, you can play with me with your fingers." It didn't take long before Anthony took off his pajamas and gently lay on top of her. Rita spread her legs and carefully guided Anthony into her. "Anthony, I love you so much. You know I have always loved you."

The next day Anthony moved into Rita's bedroom, and he gave up the living-room couch forever. Since he was underage, they both knew they had to keep their new relationship secret. As his guardian, Rita could get into big trouble.

XI

In his senior year, Anthony was once again invited to participate in the national wrestling championships. This time he did not do as well as the year before. He lost in the semifinals and wound up with a bronze medal. But he no longer had to worry about getting an athletic scholarship to pay for college. He had been recruited by most universities with an NCAA Division One wrestling team. The Princeton coach, who had been called by Coach Fritz, had come to see Anthony during several of his matches. After he saw him wrestle, he invited Anthony to come visit the university. After the visit there was no doubt in Anthony's mind; he was going to Princeton! Money would not be a problem; he had been offered a full scholarship, including room and board.

Anthony's graduation was a time of mixed emotions for Rita. On the one hand, she was bursting with pride that he graduated as the valedictorian of his class. On the other hand, she knew graduation meant that he would, at the end of the summer, be off to college. She tried to hide her dread of his leaving, but Anthony noticed.

"Don't worry, Aunt Rita, I'll still be here all summer, and Princeton is really close-by. I can come home often."

"I know, darling, but you're growing up fast, and after college you'll find your own way. You've got a great future ahead of you, and you won't want to be tied down by some old woman."

"Stop talking that way! You're not old, and I'll never feel tied down. You'll always be part of my life, no matter what I do."

"I know, darling. I know you love me very much, but you have your whole life in front of you. I know you'll be a very successful man, just like your father was, and I don't want to stand in your way."

Anthony did not like that type of talk, and he quickly changed the subject. "Coach Fritz says I can get a job at the YMCA as lifeguard and assistant wrestling coach. It sounds great, but I'll earn a lot more if I stay at the grocery store and work full time this summer. What do you think I should do?"

"The extra money would be nice for college, but with your schoolwork and your job, you have worked very hard this year. Why don't you relax a little and take the job at the Y? Besides, I have a little graduation present for you."

"You really don't have to give me a graduation present; you've done so much already."

"Well, college is expensive, and your scholarship will not cover all the extras. After your mom passed away, I opened a savings account in your name. Over the years I have been able to deposit most of your Social Security and VA money into that account. Here is the latest bank statement. It's in your name and shows a very nice little balance."

"Aunt Rita, you paid for everything, and even gave me an allowance. That money was supposed to pay my expenses. It's yours. I can't take it!"

"Anthony, don't talk nonsense; you were never a paying guest. We were and are one little household, just the two of us. I happen to be the breadwinner, so I pay the bills."

"But you've already done so much for me. I didn't realize you were paying for everything; that does not seem fair."

"Anthony, my love, it's you who has done so very much for me. You can't imagine how much you mean to me."

It was hard to see who started it, but they flew into each other's arms and started kissing heavily. "Rita, Rita, you have been so good to me, I love you very much."

"Do you realize this is the first time you called me Rita and dropped the 'Aunt'?"

"Do you mind?"

"Of course not, my darling, I love it!" Anthony scooped Rita up into his arms and carried her into the bedroom.

XII

Rita did not own a car, so, at the beginning of the school year, Rita and Anthony took the bus to Princeton. Anthony had shipped his clothes and other belongings ahead by UPS. During the summer Anthony had been told that he would be sharing a suite with three other members of the wrestling team. The university had given Anthony their names and telephone numbers, and they had already spoken on the phone.

Anthony was the last to arrive. His three suite mates had already unpacked and settled in. Rita was not sure if she would be allowed to go into the dorm to see Anthony's room and meet his roommates. She asked a young girl who was standing in front of the dorm.

"Of course parents can go up; this is move-in day."

When Anthony and Rita came into the room, the three roommates stood up to introduce themselves to Rita.

"Hi, I'm Doug Werner, and you must be Anthony's mom."

"So nice to meet you, Doug. I'm actually Anthony's aunt. His mother is no longer with us, and Anthony has been living at my house."

"I'm so sorry, ma'am, I didn't know."

"That's okay; you had no way of knowing."

Rita turned to the other boys. "And who are you?"

"I'm Timothy Winters, but I like to be called Tim, and this here is Adam Randall."

"I'm Anthony. I spoke to you guys on the phone." The conversation quickly turned to wrestling. Tim Winters had also been to the national championships and was impressed that Anthony had won a gold medal in his junior year.

"The year I won gold, I was still sixteen and competed in the cadet category at one hundred and fifty-two pounds. The following year they had me in the junior category; I couldn't get down to one sixty-three, so I had to compete in the one-eighty-five-pound group. That year I could do no better than bronze."

"Bronze, are you kidding? I wish I could have gotten that far. I only got invited to the nationals in my senior year and had a tough time getting my weight down to one forty-five. I never got to meet you because I lost in the early rounds and went home early."

"Tim, you wrestled at one forty-five? What do you weigh now?"

"I'm one hundred and fifty-one now, and this year I'll have to wrestle at one sixty-five." Neither Adam nor Doug had made it to the nationals, but they had placed high in their respective state championships. In the coming season, Adam would be wrestling at one hundred and eighty-four, and Doug would be competing at two hundred and eleven as a heavyweight.

When it became time to leave, Rita signaled Anthony that it was time for her to go. Before entering the dorm, they had agreed it would be too painful for Rita to say good-bye in front of Anthony's roommates. Instead, Rita would take Anthony to dinner in a nice restaurant in town, and after that he would bring her to the bus station for the trip home.

During most of their dinner, Rita stayed in control of her emotions; she did not want to break down in front of Anthony. But as the time to leave approached, she burst out in tears.

"Oh, Anthony, I'm going to miss you so much. The apartment will be so empty without you; I dread not being able to hold you in my arms."

"Rita, it won't be long. I'll be home for the Christmas vacation, and that is only a few short months from now. Maybe I can even come see you before that time. I'm not going overseas or to the West Coast; Princeton is only a short distance from New York City."

"I know, sweetheart, and I don't want to make it difficult for you." Rita sat silently for a while, holding Anthony's hand. Then she turned very serious.

"Anthony, I have to ask you something, and I need an honest answer. Our relationship, you know what I mean, did I do wrong by putting you in that position? Was it wrong to ask you to be my lover?"

The question surprised Anthony; he had never felt Rita forced him into anything. If anything, he was grateful for her love.

"You never forced me to do anything. You love me, and I love you. Too bad we have to be so secretive about it. Don't ever apologize for our relationship; I wanted it as much as you did."

Rita smiled at Anthony and said, "I believe you, Anthony. You really love Rita, don't you?"

They left for the bus station, and Anthony took her hand as they walked down the street. "No, don't, Anthony, you never know who might see us. We don't want trouble. Remember that when I get on the bus, you can only kiss me on the cheek and no more. In public I have to be your aunt."

XIII

When classes started, Anthony settled into a routine of going to class, studying, and practicing long hours with the wrestling team. His roommates took life less seriously and reserved time for a healthy portion of socializing. They tried to drag Anthony along to some of the weekend parties, but Anthony, who did not drink, considered those parties a drinking fest and a waste of time.

Late one Saturday night, Adam came bursting into their room and called out to Anthony, who was studying, "Hey, come quick. I have someone who is dying to meet you. You want to come downstairs? Or would you rather she comes up here to meet you?"

"What are you talking about, someone wants to meet me? What the hell for!"

"Just come downstairs, and you'll see." Anthony was curious, so he followed Adam down to the lobby where Marie, Adam's date, and Sue-Ellen Worthingham were waiting for them. Anthony had no idea who Sue-Ellen was, but she walked right up to him.

"Hi, I'm Sue-Ellen, and I have been dying to meet you." Anthony was a little baffled and hesitantly stuck out his hand. Sue -Allen continued, "When Adam told me you were one of his roommates, I insisted he introduce us." Anthony stood there looking a little silly, not quite knowing what to say.

Adam jumped in. "Anthony, we're hoping you can join us in some late-night pizza. Sue-Ellen has something special to celebrate, and she wants to treat all of us to pizza in that cozy little restaurant on Main Street."

By that time Anthony had recovered his composure, and in order not to appear rude, he agreed to go along. The four of them, Adam and his date, Sue-Ellen and Anthony, headed for Ciao Amici's. During the walk, Sue-Ellen was very talkative, telling Anthony how she heard that he was a champion wrestler, and that she had been dying to find someone to introduce him to her. Ciao Amici's was a small, intimate restaurant with several tables in the front near the bar, and some booths in the back. Adam chose a booth. Anthony waited to see where the others seated themselves; Adam and his date sat next to each other on one side of the booth, and Sue-Ellen sat on the other side. That left the spot next to Sue-Ellen open for him.

As he sat down, Sue-Ellen slid closer and gave him a big smile. On the walk over from the dorm, Anthony had not gotten a close look at Sue-Ellen.

He was a little embarrassed to study her face while they walked, and he had mostly looked straight ahead while Sue-Ellen, walking at his side, did most of the talking. Now, with her sitting so close, he managed to get a good look at her. She had a beautiful face and long dark brown hair that flowed over her shoulders. He had noticed before that she had a nice figure; now, sitting so close, he could not help noticing that she had nice breasts—maybe a little large, but very nice.

The conversation started out by discussing who was at the party that Adam and the girls had been to earlier that evening. Rather than sit and listen to that, Anthony asked Sue-Ellen to tell him more about herself. Sue-Ellen looked at him with a naughty little smile.

"So you want to know all about little old me, finally. I thought you'd never ask. Okay then, I'm a freshman here at Princeton just like you, and I come from California. I was on my high school swim team, and I was a cheerleader for our football team."

Anthony showed interest in her sports. "Do you plan to go out for either the swim team or maybe the cheerleading squad?"

"I'm not sure I'm good enough for that. I come from a small California town, and our high school was relatively small, so we never competed in state-wide events. I never really tested my skills. I do plan to try out for the golf team. After horseback riding, it's my favorite sport. I won several junior titles at our local club."

"But you like horseback riding better than golf?"

"Oh for sure; I miss my horse Misty a lot."

"You really have your own horse?" Adam asked.

"Yes, we keep several horses on the ranch, but Misty is my favorite."

This caught Adam's interest. "Don't tell me you actually live on a ranch."

"No, silly, we don't live there; my daddy has a ranch about forty miles from where we live. They keep a herd of cattle there, but mostly he has the ranch to keep his racehorses."

Anthony became even more interested. "First a ranch and now racehorses. What the heck does your father do?"

"Mostly real estate. He started out by building several shopping centers, but since that time, he has bought several hotels. We also own two resorts in the Bahamas, which have about seven hundred time-share apartments."

Adam was amazed. "You're making that up, right? At the party the guys told me your dad was rich, but this, that's unbelievable."

"Why would I lie about it? You can always google my dad and see what else he owns. Just look up Sam Worthingham, Alto Sierra Holding Company, or just Sam Worthingham Real Estate Investments."

"I'm sorry. I did not really mean to challenge you, but this is fantastic; your dad is a real celebrity." For the rest of the evening, they mostly talked about their hometowns and their high schools.

Anthony was glad no one asked details about his homelife. Adam did mention that Anthony was living with his aunt, but it was left at that. When it came to pay, Anthony noticed that Sue-Ellen pulled out a platinum American Express card. The waiter could not accept it.

"Sorry, we don't take American Express."

"That's all right," Sue-Ellen said as she placed a gold Visa card on top of the check. All three thanked her for the dinner, and Anthony asked, "What is the special occasion you are celebrating?"

Sue-Ellen giggled. "Finally meeting you." Anthony blushed from ear to ear, and Adam gave him a fist bump.

After they left the restaurant, Anthony and Adam walked the girls back to the girls' dormitory buildings. They stood outside talking for a while, and when it was time for the girls to go inside, Sue-Ellen said, "Sorry you boys can't come upstairs." Then laughingly she added, "Anyway, not tonight." As she said that, she turned to Anthony. "Mind if I give you a hug?" She put both arms around his neck and held him tight for a moment as she whispered in his year, "Here is a note with my telephone number on it. Call me. I want to see you again. Man, are you gorgeous!"

When Anthony and Adam returned to their room, their roommates Tim and Doug were sitting around talking about different people they had met that night. As Adam entered the room, Tim called out to him, "Where the hell have you been? You just left us at the party and never even said where you were going."

"You're not going to believe this, but it seems Romeo here has all kinds of special powers of attraction."

"You mean Mister Unsociable finally went out and, God forbid, actually spoke to a girl?"

"Hold on, hold on, let me tell you what happened. At the party, Marie, the girl I've been dating, introduced me to Sue-Ellen Worthingham. Do you know who that is?"

"Sure, she is that rich babe who lives with her roommate in what the other girls refer to as the Gold Coast. What about her?"

"Hold on, let me tell you the full story. After Marie introduced me, Sue-Ellen said that she had heard I was on the wrestling team. When I told her I was, she got excited and asked if I could introduce her to Anthony. She actually referred to him as 'that wrestling hunk.' I told her that would be easy, since Anthony was one of my roommates. She asked did I know where he would be hanging out, and I told her I assumed he would be in our room studying.

"She wanted to leave right then and there to meet him. I was somewhat hesitant, but Marie urged me to do it. After she met Anthony, Sue-Ellen took the three of us for pizza at Ciao Amici's. You know, that little restaurant close to here. I tell you, for the rest of the evening, she was all over Anthony. And you heard she was rich; you have no idea. Her father owns hotels, shopping centers, resorts in Bermuda, and for good measure, a ranch where he keeps his racehorses."

"And you say she had the hots for our boy Anthony?" Tim sounded a little skeptical, but Adam assured him it was true.

"You have no idea; she was all over him and made no bones about the fact that she was making a serious play for him. I have seldom seen a girl act like that. She had no trouble letting Marie and me see she was going after him in a big way."

Doug started laughing. "Anthony, you've been holding back on us. Where is this magic aftershave you must be using?" Anthony pulled up his shoulders; he had been silent while Adam described what happened between him and Sue-Ellen.

"To tell you guys the truth, I was not comfortable with the way she was behaving. Sure, she is an attractive girl, but I felt a little strange. Adam, didn't you find it a little weird the way she showed that she liked me? She knows nothing about me, and I only met her for the first time this evening."

"Attractive?" Adam jumped in. "She is gorgeous. With her looks and sexy figure, every guy in school is probably lusting after her. I'll trade places with you in a wink. Boy, what a babe, and stinking rich too."

"Okay, so you'll trade places with me just because she is pretty and says her father is filthy rich? That is pretty shallow, don't you think? You really don't know her; you also met her for the very first time this evening. By the way, Tim, what's this about her and her roommate staying in the Gold Coast?"

"Some of the guys I had lunch with last week were discussing her. Adam guessed right; a lot of the men on campus would kill for a date with her. Apparently she shares a suite with just one other girl. The other girl, Kay Goodman, is rumored to be at least as rich as Sue-Ellen. Hence, the name Gold Coast. But as I hear it, the guys are interested in Sue-Ellen and not her roommate."

Anthony found that strange. "Why is that? If they are after a rich girl, why not the roommate?"

"Seems like those two girls are like two opposites. Sue-Ellen is outgoing, the sexiest girl in our freshman class, and maybe even on campus. Kay, her roommate, is skinny, and she certainly does not have Sue-Ellen's looks."

"Is she ugly?"

"No, not that, but they said that her face is just very plain. Like Anthony here, she spends a lot of time studying and practicing her sports; she plays both volleyball and water polo."

"Is she on the university team?"

"Yeah, she is six feet two."

"Tim, you sound like you met the two of them."

"I told you I was having lunch with some guys who were discussing, or should I say drooling, over Sue-Ellen. They also talked about Kay and had a good laugh when they compared her flat chest to Sue-Ellen's ample bosom. Most of the time, they referred to her as the beanstalk whose shoulder blades are bigger than her breasts."

Anthony shook his head, indicating that type of talk was not for him. "Sounds like a lot of crap to me. I really don't know what Sue-Ellen sees in me when apparently, she can get any guy she wants."

Doug did not agree. "Don't underestimate yourself. You're darn good-looking, and I have heard a lot of girls say they find you very attractive. Even some of the guys on the wrestling team have commented that you're built like Superman. With your height, wide shoulders, and great abs, you are an imposing figure; you intimidate most of your opponents in a wrestling match. I might add that girls find that Asian look of yours very sexy."

Adam agreed with Doug. "I don't find it strange at all that Sue-Ellen finds you very attractive, but I agree with you that her approach this evening was rather strange. I think we have to think of Sue-Ellen in the sense of 'Whatever Lola wants, Lola gets.' She is probably spoiled rotten by her father, and she is used to getting her way, no matter what."

"Great, and I'm the victim!"

"Now stop it! I'm sorry I agreed to introduce you. A beautiful rich girl likes you, and you keep moaning about how she showed that this evening."

"That's not fair, Adam. Of course I am flattered to no end that she likes me, but you too were a little surprised at the way she came on to me. Don't misunderstand me, I think she is a great kid, a lot of fun to be with. I really enjoyed our little dinner."

XIV

Anthony did not call Sue-Ellen. He was much too wrapped up in his first intercollegiate wrestling match, which was to take place the next Saturday. Despite his coach's assurance that he had nothing to worry about, he was very nervous. Somehow he had convinced himself that if he did not do well in intercollegiate matches, he would lose his scholarship.

As it turned out, he had nothing to worry about. He easily won his first match and was the only one on his team to win all three of his matches. Anthony had not expected that the bleachers would be filled with supporters. When he won his first match, he heard someone cheering loudly. He looked up at the bleachers, and it was Sue-Ellen. She was surrounded by a group of her friends.

He waved back at her, and she shouted, "Great going, Anthony. You were fabulous, honey." This evoked a few comments from his teammates when he walked back to the bench. Adam was quick to straighten out the others.

"Of course she knows who he is. She's Anthony's new girlfriend." To rile the others a little, he added, "The only reason she is here is to cheer for Anthony. You don't really think a girl like that would come to see you guys."

Anthony felt Adam's teasing was going a little too far. "Sure, I know her; she is a great kid, but to call her my girlfriend is a little much. It's nice she is here. It looks like she brought a bunch of her friends to help cheer us on."

When Anthony finished his final match, Sue-Ellen stood up, clapping her hands and cheering loudly. As he headed for the locker room, she yelled loudly, so everybody in the gym could hear, "Anthony, don't forget to call me!"

The very next day, Anthony did call. It was Sunday; they did not have classes, and they arranged to have lunch and spend the afternoon together. Lunch turned out to be a two-hour event. They talked about everything and nothing. Anthony discovered that Sue-Ellen was a very interesting person. He realized he liked this girl a lot. After lunch they took a walk around the town. Then Sue-Ellen suggested they go out to Green Meadows Park. In the park they followed the long hiking trails, and Sue-Ellen hooked her arm in Anthony's as they walked along.

When they sat down on a small rustic bench along the trail, Sue-Ellen asked, "Was it bad of me to be so aggressive about getting to meet you? Some of the girls in the dorm say I acted like a real floozy. Do you think I did?"

"Was I surprised? Sure I was, but it was also very flattering. You must have noticed that at first I did not know how to react. But you, a floozy? No way!"

"Anthony, I know I came on a little too fast, but I'm not sorry; actually, I'm glad I did. The first time I saw you on campus, something inside of me stirred. You did not see me, but I could not keep my eyes off you. Don't laugh when I tell you that I sort of stalked you for a couple of days before I got Adam to introduce us. I don't know how it happens, but sometimes you see somebody, and your head spins, and you just have to be with him."

She looked at him with a nervous little smile and asked, "Do you like me, maybe just a little?"

Anthony had to laugh. "Of course I like you. I like you a lot. I would not spend all afternoon with you just to humor you. Yes, the answer is, I like you a lot and really enjoy being with you. This afternoon was really great."

Anthony started seeing a lot of Sue-Ellen. She dragged him to all the parties she was invited to. He had to admit he looked forward to being with Sue-Ellen, and he became a lot more sociable at parties. Anthony did, however, reserve a lot of his time for studying and wrestling practice. That did not always please Sue-Ellen, who also wanted to see him on weeknights. For his part Anthony was not always comfortable with the way Sue-Ellen dressed. Once at a party, he commented that the sweater she was wearing showed way too much cleavage.

In response Sue-Ellen pushed out her chest and said, "They're real. Want to feel them?"

"Come on, it's just that all the guys are staring at you."

With her characteristic sexy smile, she shot back, "That's what it's all about, silly."

Later that evening Sue-Ellen told her roommate about Anthony's comments about her sweater. "I think I'm finally getting him a little jealous. He really did not like the other guys looking at my breasts. Maybe I can finally get him to be a little more intimate with me. Dammit, he treats me like a sister, and I want to make love to the guy."

Her roommate, the one Tim had described as a beanstalk, gave her a disparaging look.

"Maybe you are a little too fast for him. The times I've met him, he seems like an awfully nice guy, and it looks like he likes you a lot. Don't push it. You might scare him away, and if you don't mind me saying so, you are a little fast. From what you told me about high school, you are very quick to have sex with a guy."

"Oh, stop the crap. I like getting laid, but I was not easy. I only did it with the biggest studs in school. Besides, what would you know? You've probably never even made out with a boy. Kissing is probably a big deal for you."

Kay Goodman stayed perfectly calm; by now she was used to having other girls make fun of her lack of sexual experience. "Okay, calm down already. All

I was saying was that maybe you should go a little slower with Anthony. He seems like a great guy. Maybe he takes sex very seriously. But it's a free world; you can do what you want. By the way, I was not criticizing what you did in high school. I just have a different take on the subject."

Sue-Ellen was already over it and continued right on. "I'd love to take him home for the Xmas vacation to show him off to all the girls at the country club. Would they be jealous or what! I asked him, but he won't come. He says he has to go see that aunt of his. You know, the one who keeps calling him. Anyway, I'll definitely invite him to California this summer."

"You know he is on scholarship; do you think he can afford it?"

"No problem. I'll buy his ticket."

"Did you ever consider he might not like that? Guys have a lot of pride; he may not want to go if he cannot afford to pay for it himself."

"Stop being so damn negative, I'll have him in my bed before you know it!"

Sue-Ellen finally got Anthony to kiss her and make out a little, but he would not go any further. When it came time to go home for Christmas vacation, she tearfully hung in his arms for quite a while.

"Darling, I'm going to miss you so much; are you sure I can't get you to come to California just for a few days? My treat?"

"I told you, honey, I've got to spend some time with my Aunt Rita, and the Christmas vacation is short enough as is."

"Yes, I understand. Here, I got you a small Christmas present." She handed him a beautifully wrapped package.

"Oh no, you don't. We didn't agree to exchange presents, and I have nothing for you!"

"Come on. If you want, you can bring me something from New York City. But here, please take it; I really want you to have it." Anthony unpacked his present and unfolded the beautiful sweater Sue-Ellen had bought him.

"Sue-Ellen, I really can't accept this; it is much too nice."

"It will look great on you, and when you wear it during Christmas, it will make you think of me." Before Anthony could offer further protests, the limousine, which Sue-Ellen had ordered to take her to Newark Airport, arrived, and Sue-Ellen had a new idea. "Darling, why don't you come with me to the airport? It's less than an hour ride, and the limo will bring you right back."

"You've got to be kidding."

"I'm serious. It won't cost anything extra, and besides, Daddy is paying anyway."

Anthony did not protest when Sue-Ellen pulled him into the limo, and they were on the way to the airport. In the comfortable backseat, Sue-Ellen snuggled up to Anthony and started making out with him. Anthony pointed to the driver in the front, and Sue-Ellen giggled.

"Don't worry; he's paid to pay attention to the road and not the backseat. Besides, he is getting a very generous tip." At the departure hall the limo waited for Anthony to help Sue-Ellen with her suitcase. After she finished checking her luggage at curbside, she kissed Anthony once more and went into the terminal. Anthony got back into the limo for the ride back to Princeton.

The next morning Anthony boarded a bus that would take him home to New York City.

XV

As Anthony was about to insert his key into the lock, the door to the apartment flew open, and Rita practically jumped into his arms. "Darling, darling, you're home! I've so been looking forward to this!" She hugged him and kissed him and finally pulled him into the apartment. Because of Rita's excitement, neither of them noticed Mrs. Babinski, their next-door neighbor, stepping out of the elevator and staring at them.

Rita had decorated the apartment for Christmas, and when Anthony noticed the presents under the Christmas tree, he was glad he had found time to buy something for Rita in a small boutique in Princeton. Rita wanted to do everything at the same time. Hug Anthony, show him the special decorations she had bought for the tree, and serve him the coffee and cake she had prepared for his arrival. She finally settled down so the two of them could sit and talk about what had happened since Anthony left for college. Even though she had called Anthony about every other day, she still had plenty of questions.

Anthony told her about almost everything, but he did not mention Sue-Ellen, and as if they had agreed on the subject, Rita did not ask about any girls he might have met. By the time they finished talking, it was dinnertime, and Rita got up to go to the kitchen.

"I hope you're hungry because I have prepared your favorite dinner for you. I have to do a few more things; come into the kitchen and talk to me." Anthony followed her into the kitchen, and it was like he had never left, with Rita busy preparing dinner and Anthony sitting at the kitchen table telling her about what happened at school. After dinner they sat for a long time closely huddled on the couch. They had turned on the TV, but neither of them paid much attention to what was on. Rita's hand was stroking the back of Anthony's neck when she suggested they go to bed.

They undressed, and Anthony lay down on the bed while Rita went to the bathroom. He was lying naked on his back when she came back into the room. When he looked at her firm, well-shaped body, he felt a little guilty. He could not help thinking about Sue-Ellen; he imagined what her naked body would look like, and in his mind, he compared her to Rita. Rita came over to the bed and gently lay down on top of Anthony. As he felt her press her body against his, all the thoughts about Sue-Ellen quickly disappeared, together with his guilty feelings.

It was almost ten in the morning by the time Anthony woke up. Rita was standing in the door looking at him.

"You should have woken me up. We were going to leave early to see the decorations on Fifth Avenue and the tree at Rockefeller Center."

"Don't worry; we have plenty of time. You really needed your sleep. We don't have to do everything in one day." She walked over to the bed. "Oh baby, I'm so happy to have you home." She took off her robe and slid back in bed with him. Their kissing quickly became more urgent, and Anthony rolled on top of her. She could feel that he was completely aroused, and she spread her legs so he could enter her.

The two of them were so involved in their love-making that they did not hear the front door open. Not until they heard a terrible shriek did they look up and see Mrs. Babinski standing in their bedroom doorway. Anthony jumped up and grabbed the sheet in order to cover Rita, but Mrs. Babinski had already run out the front door.

Rita was crying uncontrollably. "We were so careful. How could this happen?" she sobbed. Anthony was pretty shook up too, but he was the first to regain his composure. He tried desperately to calm Rita down.

"Don't worry. I'll talk to her; I'll explain to her that we love each other." But Rita could not be consoled.

"It won't work; that bitch will make trouble and go to the police." She burst out crying again. "Oh, what have I done, what have I done? Anthony, they'll come and take you away from me." Anthony took her into his arms and gently tried to encourage her by telling her that Mrs. Babinski would probably not go to the police since she had no business sneaking into their apartment like that.

"Oh yes, I know her; she will love going to the police. We probably forgot to lock the door, and she could walk right in without us noticing." It took a long time to calm Rita enough to persuade her that both of them should get dressed and straighten up the bedroom, in case Mrs. Babinski did go to the police. Maybe they could claim nothing happened, that Mrs. Babinski was lying because she hated Rita? After all, it was her word against the two of them. No matter what Anthony came up with, Rita was convinced Mrs. Babinski would go to the police, and they would take Anthony away from her.

It was a little after two in the afternoon when they heard the dreaded knock on the door. Anthony went to open it. A man in street clothes was standing in front of the door, and two uniformed policemen were standing behind him.

"Is Miss Rita Thomson home?" Anthony did not answer, but the man could see Rita standing behind him. He pushed past Anthony and asked Rita, "Are you Rita Thomson?" Rita was very frightened, but held her own.

"Who are you, and what gives you the right to barge into my apartment like this?"

"I'm a member of the New York City Police sex crime investigating unit. You know us as the vice squad. You have been accused of having sex with a minor. I have to ask you to come with me; we would like to question you about it."

Anthony jumped in. "We did nothing wrong. She does not have to go with you. Just leave her alone and get out of here."

"Please come with me willingly. I don't what to get an arrest warrant and force you to come with us."

"Why don't you just ask your questions here?" Rita said. "I have nothing to hide."

"Sorry, ma'am, I have to ask you to come to the station so we can take your statement, and it would be helpful if this young man comes along too. We would also like to talk to him."

"Mrs. Babinski called you, didn't she? She hates me!"

"Please, ma'am, just come to the station. We'll explain why we want to question you."

"All right, we'll come, but we are not getting into a police squad car. We'll come by taxi."

"I understand how you feel, ma'am. I have an unmarked car, and the officers will not go with us. They were here to protect me in the event someone got angry and attacked me. I am happy that in your case, that is not a problem."

At the police station, Rita and Anthony were ushered into separate rooms. Before they were separated, Anthony told Rita not to say anything without first asking for a lawyer. Two detectives entered the little room in which Rita had been placed.

"Hi, I am Detective Kelly, and this is my partner, Frank Johnson. We're here to tell you why you were brought in for questioning, and we would like to hear what you have to say about it. To start with, let me read from a sworn statement given to us by a Mrs. Babinski. You do know Mrs. Babinski, don't you?" Rita answered affirmatively, and the detective started to read:

"I'm Mrs. Karina Babinski, and I live at One-One-Five-One Third Avenue, Apartment Four-Seven-Seven in New York City. Miss Rita Thomson lives on the same floor. Anthony and his mother used to live next door to Miss Thomson, and she was his mother's best friend. When Anthony's mother died, Miss Thomson became his guardian, and he moved in with her. From the beginning, I felt things were all wrong. Even while his mother was still alive, she hovered over Anthony, and she used to hug and kiss him all the time. When he grew a little older, this continued. But he wasn't a little boy anymore, so it should have stopped. I discussed this with my friend Mrs. Kane, who lives in the same apartment complex and has the apartment facing Miss Thomson's. Mrs. Kane told me that from her apartment, she could see into the living room of Miss Thomson's apartment. She too was suspicious of Miss Thomson's relation to the boy.

"She told me that when Anthony first moved in, she could see him preparing to go to bed. He used to pull the coffee table away from the front of the couch and convert the couch to a bed. Before he undressed, he would carefully pull the curtains. This was his standard routine, until one night the curtains stayed open, and the coffee table and couch remained as they were. After that the curtains stayed open every night. Since the apartment only has one bedroom, Mrs. Kane knew that Anthony must be sleeping in Miss Thomson's bedroom. She called Child Protective Services, but they never really checked. Last night when I came home, I saw Miss Thomson and the boy in a lover's embrace in front of their apartment. As a Christian woman, I felt this was wrong and I should do something about it.

"This morning I went over to tell Miss Thomson that we suspected what was going on and that this behavior had to stop. When I knocked on the door, no one answered, but I felt that the door was unlocked. When I entered the apartment, I saw no one, and when I went into the hallway looking for her, I saw the two of them having intercourse on her bed. I left immediately, and since I had actually seen them having sex, I knew I had to report this to the police."

After he finished reading Mrs. Babinski's statement, the detective turned to Rita, who was sitting with her head down, staring at her hands.

"Do you want to comment on Mrs. Babinski's statement?" Rita kept her head down and said nothing. "She says she saw you have intercourse with the young man she referred to as Anthony. She also says you are his guardian. Is this true?"

Finally Rita spoke up. "I'd like to see a lawyer."

"Okay, you don't have to answer; we can look that up pretty quick. If the kid turns out to be your ward, you'll definitely need a lawyer."

While the detectives were questioning Rita, a female detective questioned Anthony in another room. "You are Anthony Walker, is that correct?"

Anthony was quite hostile. "I don't have to tell you anything. You have no right bringing us here. We did absolutely nothing wrong."

"That's what I'm here to find out, but you'll have to help me. Let's start from the beginning. You are Anthony Walker, seventeen years old, and you live on Third Avenue in the apartment of a Miss Rita Thomson. Is that right?" Anthony nodded his head yes. "Now, can you tell me what happened this morning that made Mrs. Babinski come to us?"

"That woman hates us, and she is always lying about us."

"Do you think that just because she is lying, she would go to the police and tell them that she saw you and Miss Thomson having intercourse?"

"She's lying; I told you she hates us."

"That's what we're trying to find out. She did give a sworn statement, and we have to investigate."

"I want to talk to my aunt."

"I don't know if that is possible right now; I would have to check with my colleagues. I am afraid she will have to stay here tonight. A judge will have to decide if, based on Mrs. Babinski's statement, she will have to stand trial or not."

Anthony jumped to his feet. "You can't do that, she did nothing wrong. Mrs. Babinski is lying."

"Sit down, son. I understand you want to protect her, but we have more people who will testify that you and your aunt, who is not really your aunt, have had sexual relations."

Anthony was stunned; he could not imagine who else had ever seen Rita and him making love. "That can't be true. That is impossible!"

"I am sorry, but it is true. Others have seen what was going on between the two of you. We're in the process of getting their statements right now." Anthony was determined to get Rita out of this.

"It's all my fault," he blurted out. "I started it. I just came home from college, and this morning I went into her bedroom to say good morning and tell her I was up. I forgot to knock, and when I went in, she was standing there naked. Rather than leave the room, I went up to her and started kissing her. She told me to stop and leave the room, but I persisted and kept kissing her and putting my hands all over her body. I was very excited, and I put her on the bed and made love to her. She could not help it. It was all my doing!"

"Anthony, it's very noble of you to try and take the blame, but unless you raped her, she is responsible. We know she is your guardian."

"I did force her! I'm much stronger, and she could not hold me off."

"Anthony, it will not help her if you start lying about what was going on. Mrs. Babinski saw you, and your aunt was not struggling to get away. All indications are that she was an active participant. Besides, as I said, we have other witnesses who will testify that it happened before."

Anthony broke down crying.

XVI

The next day Rita met with a lawyer, and they prepared for her arraignment before a local magistrate. The district attorney's office introduced three more sworn statements, besides those from Mrs. Babinski and Mrs. Kane, from persons who claimed to have reason to believe that Rita had maintained a sexual relationship with Anthony. The magistrate had no trouble binding Rita's case over for trial. Afterward, Rita's lawyer explained to her that the DA had a more-or-less open-and-shut case, and there was little they could offer in defense.

"On the one hand, you are lucky they can only prove one incident of sexual contact between the two of you while the boy was already seventeen. If they could prove you had sex with him before that, they would have also charged you with statutory rape. But it is still a difficult case. As his guardian you are deemed to be an officer of the court and are charged with the welfare of your ward. There are statutes that hold that an adult person who has intercourse with a minor who is his or her adopted child, stepchild, foster child, or ward—and is at the time of the intercourse, living with that person as a member of the family—is liable on conviction.

"I think it will be possible to have the court put aside all the witnesses' testimony except that of Mrs. Babinski. We could try to disprove her testimony simply on the grounds that she hates you. But you never know what the jury will do. They might look at Anthony and decide he is more of a man than a boy, and the fact that you had sex with him is no big deal. In that case they might find you not guilty. All I can say is that I'll fight like hell for you.

"To me, Anthony looks like a grown man who no longer needs your protection. For God's sake, he is a college freshman. Whatever happened between the two of you is your business, and the state should stay out of it. The stupid thing about all this is that, if it had happened a few months later, Anthony would have been eighteen, no longer your ward, and the two of you would have been free to do whatever."

Rita wanted to know if it would be hard to try and prove that Mrs. Babinski was lying in telling what she saw.

"It certainly won't be easy. I would have to put you as well as Anthony on the stand, and both of you under oath would have to declare that you never had intercourse and that she made up her testimony solely because she hates you. I have to warn you, the trial would be a media circus; the public loves a sex trial, and the newspapers would cover every detail, especially what Mrs. Babinski says she saw."

"I don't want to put Anthony through all that. Is there any other way you can solve this for me?"

"I could try to get the DA to offer us a plea bargain."

"That would prevent a trial and Anthony having to be questioned in public?"

"Yes, if we accept what the DA offers, you would not go to trial. A judge would sentence you to whatever we had agreed upon with the DA."

"Please see what you can do."

The newspapers picked up the story and had a ball with it. The so-called scandal sheets tried to outdo each other with juicy headlines like, "Guardian Creates Love Nest with Ward." Or "Fifty-Two-Year-Old Model Seduces Seventeen-Year-Old Ward." Or "Fifty-Something Woman Keeps In-House Boy Toy." Or better yet, "Minor and Guardian Live Like Husband and Wife." The barrage of newspaper stories continued for days, with each paper trying to produce more details, until finally Mrs. Babinski secretly sold a copy of her sworn testimony to a Manhattan weekly and embellished it with some graphic details that she made up.

The DA's office discovered more evidence against Rita that seriously jeopardized her case. Her previous conviction and jail time should have disqualified her from being appointed as Anthony's guardian. They had a choice of presenting this during a trial and increasing the chance of a conviction with a pretty harsh sentence. But at the same time, they would expose a serious failure of the judicial system in appointing her as his guardian. To put an end to all the publicity surrounding the case, they quickly offered a deal.

Rita's lawyer did not accept the first offer and bargained hard to get a better deal for her. The final plea seemed harsh to Rita, but she accepted it to prevent a trial. It called for a three-year jail sentence with the possibility of parole after twenty-four months. The lawyer did manage to have it specified that jail time would be spent in the so-called "Farm," the nickname for the minimum-security women's prison where mostly white-collar criminals were sent. Probably one of the hardest parts for Rita was that the sentence forbade her from any contact whatsoever with Anthony until he was twenty-one. Rita's lawyer was sure that was excessive and that he could get that changed as soon as Anthony became eighteen and would be considered an adult. A few days after sentencing, Rita was processed in Queens. Soon thereafter she was shipped off to the prison in Upstate New York.

During sentencing Rita had been stripped of her guardianship; Anthony automatically became a ward of the court. The judge noted that he was enrolled in college, and since he would be eighteen in three months, he was instructed to return to Princeton on his own recognizance.

Contrary to the instructions of the judge, Anthony did not return to school. Instead, he returned to the apartment. After three days the super came to warn him that he could not stay; he had to vacate the apartment. Anthony refused, and the super explained that he would be evicted if he didn't leave.

"Anthony, it's not up to me, but the apartment has already been assigned to another person, and I have to clear out Rita's stuff. Look, I'm on your side; I think the whole thing is stupid. For Rita to have to go to jail is crazy. What you two did is not so abnormal. You're a good-looking guy, and of course, you were attracted to her. She is one hell of a nice-looking dame. She was always real nice to me, and I sort of had a crush on her. To tell you the truth, I might even be a little jealous of you."

No matter how the super pleaded with him, Anthony would not return to school, and he stayed holed up in the apartment. Not sure how to handle the situation, the super contacted Coach Fritz, whom he had met when he joined Rita at one of Anthony's wrestling matches.

The next day Coach Fritz arrived. He brought with him Coach Kassel, the Princeton wrestling coach. The two of them made it very clear that Anthony owed it to himself and to Rita not to throw away his future by refusing to return to college. They explained that neither of them blamed Anthony for what had happened, and they were careful not to condemn Rita. The Princeton coach admitted that things would be tough for a while.

"The newspapers sensationalized the whole situation. They always think they can sell more newspapers by creating shocking headlines. But the truth is that most people have already forgotten those headlines by the next day. Anthony, we want you back at Princeton! You're a great wrestler, a fine student, and I, for one, do not think any less of you than I did the day you left for Christmas vacation."

Coach Fritz pitched in by telling Anthony how proud his mom would have been to know he was doing so well at a famous university. He also touched on the fact that everybody had been glad that Rita had taken such good care of him after his mother died, and because of her care, he now had a great future ahead of him. Finally, Anthony gave in and agreed to return to college with Coach Kassel. Coach Fritz promised to take care of closing the apartment and putting all of Rita's belongings in storage.

XVII

To his surprise, Anthony's roommates treated him like a conquering hero. Especially Adam.

"Man, you've really been holding back on us. Here we thought you were a virgin, and all along you were banging that lady. I saw a picture of her in the newspaper; she looked like quite a dish. How does a guy get so lucky? I wish I could have had something like that." Anthony got mad at the way they went on about his relationship with Rita.

"Cut it out, it wasn't like that at all. The newspapers made up most of it. They just made up something sensational, so they could sell more papers. Rita is a fine lady. She took care of me when my mom died; I had no one else to turn to. Now please stop; I don't want to hear any more about it."

But his roommates would not let up. Tim had a different view of things than Brian and Adam.

"Maybe you should have been a little less chummy with that gal, Sue-Ellen, since you had a nice thing going back home."

Doug would have none of that. "Don't be silly. I date all the time, even though I have my steady gal back home in Wisconsin."

Adam was curious. "Do you have sex with your dates here?"

"When I get a chance, why not?"

"Would you mind if your gal back home had sex with other guys while you were at school?"

"Don't be stupid, Tim, of course I would mind."

"That seems pretty hypocritical; it's okay for you but not for her."

"But it's different. She is a girl, and it is not okay. I could not accept her having sex with another guy, but girls sort of expect guys to have sex whenever they can. Besides, they blame the other girl anyway." Anthony had heard enough. He grabbed his books and headed for the library.

Anthony was expecting Sue-Ellen to contact him, but when she had not called for several days, he decided to call her. It turned out to be a big mistake. Sue-Ellen was mad as hell.

"I don't want you to call me!"

"I just called to see if we could go somewhere and have a cup of coffee or something."

"No, I don't want to see you, not now or ever again. How could you, carrying on with your aunt like that?"

"She's not my aunt!"

"Whatever, but you did fuck that woman. What the two of you did was disgusting." Sue-Ellen hung up the phone.

Kay, Sue-Ellen's roommate, heard her outburst. "You know you're wrong speaking like that to him."

"Wrong? What do you mean, wrong? How dare he call me. I read copies of the New York papers. What he and that so-called aunt of his did was just plain disgusting. It's like incest."

"Oh, cut it out. She is not related to him in any way, and he is almost eighteen, in which case nobody would have said a thing about it."

"Look, he was dating me while having an affair with that woman; no wonder he had to hurry home to NY instead of coming with me to California."

"It's a question who was dating whom. If I remember, you were all over him and complaining he would not go to bed with you. As a matter of fact, he was being a real gentleman. No matter how you tried, he would not have sex with you while he was sleeping with another woman."

"Gentleman, my ass. He was fucking that older woman he was living with."

"And you should talk. From what you told me, you're no virgin either, and you were not very discriminating as to whom you jumped in bed with."

The telephone call with Sue-Ellen had a deadly effect on Anthony. He withdrew within himself and spent all his time in the library studying. He even skipped wrestling practice, and Coach Kassel had to find him in the library to convince him to come back to practice. The constant banter of his roommates, mostly about his sex with Rita, became too much for Anthony; he requested the dean of students to assign him to another dorm room.

Anthony's new roommate was Jamal Griffin, a six-foot-ten basketball player who, like Anthony, was on full scholarship. It was Jamal who managed to talk some sense into Anthony's head. After he noticed that Anthony hardly spoke to anyone and spent all his time in the library, he confronted him.

"I don't care what you did! In the hood, where I come from, a lot of young dudes get it on with older women. Hell, they sometimes get presents from these dames, like expensive sport shoes and such. Nobody thinks much of it. People have learned to mind their own business and not go poking around to see what others are doing. I myself have made it with a few older women; as long as they were hot, I didn't care what age they were. You should only care about what good people say, the ones who care about you. To hell with all those busybodies. If I got upset every time some asshole makes a racist remark or uses the word *nigger*, I would have to leave this place and go to an all-black college."

Rooming with Jamal helped Anthony regain much of his self-respect. The two of them were the college's big jocks, and they became close friends. Anthony attended every basketball game to cheer for Jamal, and Jamal in turn did the same for Anthony at wrestling matches. When it looked like Jamal would become academically ineligible and be dropped from the basketball team, Anthony offered to help him. At first Jamal declined; he felt it would take away too much from Anthony's own studies. Anthony brushed that argument aside. He explained he had helped kids with their homework while he was in high school, and he enjoyed tutoring. He could easily spare the time. It turned out that Anthony was a very good tutor, and Jamal was much smarter than he himself thought. In high school he had always been pushed through because of his athletic ability, and he had never really taxed his brain. The two of them discovered that Jamal was actually pretty bright; he only had to learn how to study and use his time better.

One day Anthony was having lunch when Kay Goodman, Sue-Ellen's roommate, came over to where he was sitting. "Mind if I join you?"

"Fine, but do you want to be seen talking to me?"

"Anthony, I'm not Sue-Ellen. I understand the situation. I don't blame you, nor do I judge that woman. As a matter of fact, Sue-Ellen and I have had a lot of arguments about the way she treated you, and our relationship is somewhat strained at the moment."

"Sue-Ellen wasn't all wrong. I've thought about it a lot. What I did was wrong. Rita did a lot for me, and I should have controlled the situation better."

"You have to stop beating yourself up about this. You were just a confused kid whose single-parent mother had just died when this Rita lady took you in. She was all you had. Of course you love her. Besides, you were no longer a young kid when your relationship grew a little too intimate. It happened. It's over. It's unfortunate that Rita has to spend some time in jail when her only crime was loving you too much. A lot of people disagree with it, but that happens when the law is applied indiscriminately. Your case should never have gone to court."

Anthony said nothing for a while. He just looked at Kay, trying to determine if she was serious about what she was saying. Finally he responded. "I appreciate what you're saying, I really do, but it's Rita who has to sit in jail while I am free to go to college. It's hard to sit here fat, dumb, and happy while she is in jail."

"It speaks to your character that you feel it's wrong that Rita got punished while the court protected you. However, she was the adult, and as your guardian, the court made her responsible for your welfare. According to the law, you were too young to make a mature decision, so she was held responsible for what happened between the two of you."

"She never forced me to do anything against my will!"

"I accept that. Now, can we change the subject? How about telling me all about those championships you've won."

They talked about a lot more than just Anthony's wrestling. They were so involved in their conversation that Anthony misjudged the time and missed his afternoon class.

"Christ, it's three o'clock. We have been here for more than two hours. I missed my class, and it's almost time to go to wrestling practice."

Kay laughed. "I didn't realize it was getting so late. I really enjoyed talking to you." Anthony looked at her smiling face, and he did not see the plain face his roommate Tim had described.

"Mind if I tell you that you have a great smile?"

"Mind, are you nuts? I love to hear it. I don't get that many compliments and certainly not from a good-looking fellow. Pity, but it's time to go. Hurry up, or you'll be late for practice, and it will be my fault."

During the next few days, Anthony kept thinking about Kay, but she had not asked him to call. He was not sure if she wanted him to call. He mentioned it to Jamal, who was quite blunt about it.

"Of course you call her. Sounds like she is a great gal, not like that bitchy roommate of hers. Girls like that don't go around telling you to call them. Hell, man, you're the guy. You like her, you call her." But once again wrestling distracted Anthony. The NCAA Intercollegiate Wrestling Matches were coming up. Coach wanted Anthony to compete in two weight classes: at 197 pounds and also in the heavyweight class. Anthony did not have that much experience wrestling above his weight, and he spent a lot of time practicing with Doug, who by now weighed over 220 pounds.

The intercollegiate competition turned out to be a great success for Princeton. The team placed first, which was in no small part due to Anthony's achievements. He won gold in both weight classes he competed in. To celebrate the team's success, Coach Kassel organized a dinner party. Anthony was not pleased when he found out he was expected to bring a date. He asked Jamal if it would look funny if he was the only one at the dinner without a date. Jamal could not understand why his friend was so hesitant to invite a girl to the dinner.

"Bro you sure know how to make a problem out of everything. Invite that girl Kay, the one you like but never called. You can invite her, unless she is black, of course."

"That's not funny; I don't like jokes like that!"

"You're right, I'm sorry, I was out of line. You do not deserve me making that type of remark about you."

"Remarks like that show that no matter what you say, you do have a chip on your shoulder about being black in this mostly white college."

"Yup, the two of us have a chip on our shoulder. I reckon that's why we are such good friends."

Anthony did follow Jamal's advice and invited Kay to come with him to the dinner. Kay appeared shocked. "Me? You want to bring me to the wrestling dinner?"

"Yes, that's what I called to ask you. Don't you want to go?"

"Yes, of course I would love to go with you; it's just that guys don't usually ask me out. Certainly not campus sport heroes like you."

"That's ridiculous. I'd be proud to have you as my date. I think you are a great person, certainly the nicest gal I've met since I came to Princeton." Kay regained some of her composure.

"I'm flattered beyond belief, and I'd be thrilled to go. To tell you a secret, I was hoping you might call me. Not for a real date, but just to talk. Are you sure you want me as your date? The dinner is a really big deal, and all your teammates will be there."

"Do I have to come over and get on my knees?"

"Anthony, you can't imagine how happy this makes me. I'm floating on air. What should I wear?"

"Just ask the other girls. They'll know."

"Are you kidding? They won't even believe that you asked me."

After the wrestling dinner, Anthony and Kay were seen together quite frequently. When he felt that the relationship between the two of them was becoming deeper than a casual friendship, Jamal took it upon himself to talk to Kay. He asked her to join him for some coffee so they could discuss Anthony.

As soon as she sat down, Kay asked, "What's happened to Anthony? What do you have to tell me?"

"Don't worry, nothing happened to Anthony; he is fine. I just wanted to talk to you about your relationship with him."

Kay was confused. "You want to talk about our relationship? Why? What possible concern could you have about our relationship? If you must know, I like him a lot, and that is about all I'll say about it."

"I understand. You think I'm just being a busy-body trying to interfere, but that is really not the case. Hear me out, and I'll explain. It's like this: you must understand that Anthony is my main man. Probably the best friend I have ever had. His loyalty is something I have never experienced before from someone who is not part of my immediate family. As a matter of fact, my mom joked that he probably did not notice I am black.

"Anyway, the point is that Anthony carries deep scars from things that happened in the past. I don't only mean the obvious thing that most people here on campus have heard about. It's also from the fact that Anthony's own dad didn't let anybody know that Anthony even existed. And his mom got no respect because she was making it with a married man. Anthony was devoted to his mother, but he lost her at an early age. After that, he attached his loyalty to Rita, the person who took him in and provided a good home for him. As you know, that came to a cruel end.

"Kay, I think you know all this and understand how this has affected him. But what you don't know is that he is starting to fixate on you. This guy needs a female figure who is his confidante. Don't worry, he does not have a mother complex. He just needs a female whom he can trust and who is totally on his side, no matter what. In return, I think he has this need to be totally loyal to this person. He grew up in a sort of 'us against the rest of the world' mentality, and he is starting to let you into his world."

Kay took a while to absorb what Jamal was saying. "Yes, I understand that with what he has had to experience, he is somewhat skeptical toward others. I am fully aware that his mother and Rita were extremely close to him and that he relied a lot on their support while he was finding his way in a world that looked down on him because of his birth. But what makes you think he considers me more than just a friend?"

"Look, I know; we are very close friends, and I am probably the only one who he trusts with his real feelings about things. He talks to me about you."

"He talks about me?"

"Not only does he talk about you, but he is starting to have deep feelings for you."

Kay blushed. "I'll be honest with you, I am crazy about the guy, but I have never flaunted it. I am afraid that if I crowd him too much with my feelings for him, I will drive him away. Actually, I have always hoped that he and I could become more serious, but if you look at him and me, that is not very realistic."

"You might not think it's realistic. But I can tell you the guy is very serious about you, and that is why I wanted to talk to you. Anthony is starting to fall for you; actually, he already has, but has not fully come to grips with it. But I have to warn you, if the two of you get together, you can't back out. Once he drops his guard and confides in you, you can't let him down. I don't think this guy can survive a third time losing the person who is very special to him. If I sound melodramatic, so be it, but I assure you I will not stand by and see my friend hurt again!"

"You mean that, don't you? You are serious about this."

"Yes, I am, totally."

"Also about the part that he really likes me?"

"Of course, that's what it is all about. The guy is crazy about you."

Kay had tears in her eyes. "You really like him, don't you? You're really a great friend."

"I love the guy, and I can't stand to see him getting hurt again."

Kay whispered softly but Jamal heard her quite clearly say, "I too love him. I love him a lot, and I swear I'll never hurt him."

Jamal reached across the table and shook Kay's hand. "We understand each other, and we have a deal. Remember, this little meeting never took place."

"Anthony is very lucky to have a great friend like you. Sure, this meeting never took place, but I'll always remember the way you watch out for the guy I love."

Anthony had arranged to stay in Princeton for the summer, and Coach Kassel had helped him get a job in Butler College Dining, the school cafeteria, which would be open for the summer session. When Kay learned he would stay by himself in Princeton, she invited him to visit her and her family for the Fourth of July weekend. Anthony wasn't sure. First, he explained that it would be rather complicated for him to get back and forth to Deal, where she lived. Kay was quick to wipe that problem away.

"I'll come pick you up, and of course, I'll bring you back."

"I don't want you spending the holiday driving back and forth just to get me."

"Hey, it's Deal, New Jersey, less than fifty miles from here; that's less than an hour each way. Anthony, do come, we'd have so much fun, and I'm dying to introduce you to my parents. Don't worry, no strings. It would just be nice for you to meet them." Anthony was not sure, but he did not say no, and he promised to think about it.

Thinking it over meant discussing it with Jamal. After patiently listening to all the objections Anthony could think of, Jamal was still very much in favor of Anthony accepting the invitation.

"Of course you should go. It sounds like a great idea. What else do you plan to do for the Fourth, sit in your dorm room or maybe come visit me in the hood? Mind you, you are always welcome, and some-day I will introduce you to my folks, but Deal sounds like a much-better deal. Sorry that sounds funny, but seriously, don't be stupid. Just accept."

"I don't know. She just feels sorry for me that I'll be here all by myself. Anyway, I think she is so nice to me because she feels sorry for me for what happened."

"Boy, are you blind! Sure, she feels sorry for you, but that girl really loves you, and that goes a lot deeper than just feeling sorry for you. She is hurt-ing for you, for the way some assholes treat you and whisper behind your back. This girl is one of the good ones. She is the real thing. Some stupid guys call her the Beanstalk, but what do they know? It's not looks, it's character that really counts."

"I don't think she is a beanstalk. I think she is rather nice looking."

Jamal burst out laughing. "Why don't you just admit that you like this girl much more than just a little and take her up on the invitation for the Fourth?"

"All right, already, you win; I'll go."

Jamal stopped laughing and turned serious. "Anthony, I'm glad for you. I hope that someday I'll meet a girl like Kay, instead of just those lightweights who want to be seen with a jock."

XVIII

They arranged that Kay would come and get him two days before the Fourth of July weekend. Anthony was packed and ready when Kay knocked on his dorm room. When she entered the room, Kay threw her arms around him and gave him a big hug.

"Anthony, we're going to have such a good time! Do you mind if I tell you that I missed you a whole lot?"

"I don't mind. I like to hear it, and to tell you the truth, I've been looking forward to this weekend ever since you left for home."

"Okay, let's not waste any time; my car is parked very near here."

When they reached Kay's car, Anthony asked, "This red Mustang is yours?"

"Come on, don't make a big deal of it. Daddy loves me, and he likes to show off a little, so he bought me this car. I love it. Please don't be put off about it."

"Not at all. I mean, it's a beautiful car. It was really more of a compliment."

"There are more things you might have to get used to. My dad has been very successful, and he loves to show it. Please don't let it come between us."

"Of course not. I have been aware that you were not exactly poor. The only thing that makes me uneasy is that your folks might think I'm after your money."

"Anthony, stop it! I'm not stupid. I know when a guy has an eye on my father's fortune. You don't, and I never thought you did. My parents trust my judgment and won't think of you in that way. Now that we have gotten that out of the way, let's enjoy ourselves, shall we? I have looked forward to our weekend together for too long to spoil it with such silly talk. Okay, I'm rich, live with it! I hope I've got a few other compensating features."

"You sure do, or I would not be so crazy about you! But what I said is not that crazy, and I'm glad you know that I like you for what you are, not what you have. I want you to be sure of that."

"You're probably the most honest person I know. With you, it's what you see is what you get. That is why I said a little prayer hoping you would ask me out again after that wrestling dinner. Actually, it was a very big prayer."

"Believe it or not, it was I who had to worry if you liked me or not. Your biggest fault is that you underestimate yourself."

"Not really. In high school the boys were quick in teaching me the truth. I'll tell you one dark secret about myself. You're the only one I would trust with this. I never had a real date until the time you asked me to the dinner. Going out in groups, sure, but I didn't even have a date for my junior prom; and Dad arranged a date for my senior prom. He was a twenty-four-year-old who worked at my father's company. It was awkward for both of us."

Anthony leaned over and asked, "Can I kiss you?"

Kay threw her arms around him. "Finally. I've been dying to kiss you, but I didn't dare ask." She put her arms around him, and they kissed for a long time. They did not look up until someone honked at them and gave them the thumbs-up. They had almost forgotten they were sitting in a convertible parked on a public street. They both burst out laughing.

"Let the world know!" Anthony said.

"Yes," Kay said. "Let them all know! What a great way to start off our weekend."

They had so much to talk about that the trip to Deal did not seem long at all. Anthony had fully expected that Kay's parents would have a nice house, but what he saw when they arrived amazed him. An ornate entrance led them to a circular driveway. The house itself was huge; Anthony had never seen a house that large before. A short distance across carefully manicured lawns, he could see tennis courts and what looked like a swimming pool.

When they got out of the car, Kay asked laughingly, "Well, what do you think? Now that you have seen where we live, are you going to stop seeing me?"

"Now it's your turn to stop. But I am amazed. I've never seen anything like it."

"I told you Daddy is not shy about his success. Come inside, and I'll show you the rest."

Inside, they were met by Kay's parents. Kay's father was about Anthony's height—not fat, but a lot heavier than Anthony. He was wearing an outrageously loud Hawaiian shirt, and he sported a dark tan. Kay's mother, on the other hand, was dressed stylishly, but modestly. She was almost the same height as her husband. Kay had told Anthony that her mother, before she married her dad, had been Miss New Jersey and a well-known model. Anthony thought she had not aged much and that she should have been Miss America.

Kay was the first to speak. "Mom, Dad, this is my friend Anthony."

"Anthony, we're so glad you could come," Kay's mother said. "We have heard a lot about you, and now we finally get to meet you."

Kay's father extended his hand and added to his wife's welcome. "Yes, it's sure nice to have you visit us. As my wife said, our Kay has told us a lot about you, and of course we were curious. Well, she did not exaggerate."

"Daddy, stop teasing, you're embarrassing us. Anthony, don't mind what he says; he is just trying to get under my skin." She turned to her father. "You're not the only one in this house who has good taste; maybe I inherited it."

Her father laughed at her. "Touché. Clever response. Sorry, Anthony, for this banter. I hope you can take it in jest. My daughter was excited about your visit, and I am always glad to see her happy. Welcome. I'm really happy you came, and I hope we can make your stay with us a pleasant one."

Kay took Anthony around to see the rest of the house. "My aunt and her family are also coming. She and her husband will sleep in the guest room. You and my cousins will be staying in the guesthouse."

"Guesthouse?"

"Yeah, I'll show you. It's right behind the house, above the garage." They went outside to a large garage that could easily hold six cars. Above this garage were three bedrooms, each with its own bathroom. They went upstairs, and Kay chose the largest room for Anthony.

"I think you'll be comfortable here."

"Since it is about twice the size of the dorm room I have been staying in, I'm sure I'll be comfortable."

"Put your stuff down, and let's take a walk on the grounds." First they went to see the gazebo, which had a built-in bandstand. Next Kay took him to the tennis courts, and from there they went to the pool area. The Olympic-size pool was surrounded by a large area for sunbathing. Stone benches encircled an elaborate barbeque pit. Behind this area was the pool house, which contained four dressing rooms.

"Next you're going to tell me that you have your own golf course," Anthony said.

"Actually, it's not a full course, but Dad did have them build a putting green behind the flower gardens. He likes to practice his putting."

"I think I'm overwhelmed."

"Don't worry, that's it. There is no more."

"You seem very matter-of-fact about all this."

"Yes, maybe I am a little, but don't forget I grew up with all this. I forgot to tell you I'm a spoiled brat."

"I don't think you are; you never act that way."

"But I am. I am the only child of a father who likes to show his success, and I am often the beneficiary of that."

"Look, I know what spoiled brats are like, and you are not like that. Not at all."

"I'm glad you feel that way, because I despise the way some of the kids from around here go around like they own the world."

By the time they got back to the house, Kay's aunt and her family had arrived. Her kids were high school seniors. They were twins, and the girl resembled Kay's mom. Her twin brother looked a lot like her, but in a masculine way. They had all heard about Anthony and were pleased to meet him. After everybody got settled in, they gathered around the pool area for drinks. The twins were quite impressed with Anthony, and they had a barrage of questions about his wrestling. They especially wanted to know what it was like to go to the national championships. Kay's mother was enjoying the way her sister was throwing admiring glances at Anthony. Finally she had something to rival her sister's beautiful twins.

Kay's aunt and her family were tired from the trip, and they retired soon after dinner. Anthony and Kay joined her father and mother in the library for coffee. When Kay and her mother left to look at some project her mother was working on, Kay's father asked Anthony to stay so the two of them could have a talk without the girls.

"Don't worry, I won't cross examine you. But Kay is our only child and I hardly know you. It's obvious my daughter is quite taken by you. However, she has not been out in the world on her own very much. As her father I like to know who she is seeing. So tell me a little more about yourself and how you got to meet our Kay."

"I appreciate your concern sir, and I'll be happy to tell you more about myself." At first this scared Anthony a little; what could he possibly talk about with this well-known businessman? Sure, the man was very nice to him, but Anthony was still in awe of him.

To Anthony's surprise Kay's dad was very easy to talk to. He seemed interested in Anthony's studies. After a while Anthony relaxed and enjoyed talking to this man, who was knowledgeable on a variety of subjects, yet seemed to respect Anthony's opinion on the topics they discussed. They were so engrossed in their discussions that they did not realize it had gotten pretty late and everybody else had already gone to bed. When Anthony said good night and headed for the guesthouse, he realized he really liked Kay's father.

The next day was the Fourth of July, and because Kay's mother had arranged her traditional Fourth of July dinner for about thirty guests, an early brunch was served on the patio right outside the dining room. After brunch the whole group gathered at the tennis court for a friendly competition. When they chose teams, Anthony held back and said he was still a little tired and preferred to watch for a while.

Kay immediately noticed that Anthony felt ill at ease and called out to him, "I don't feel quite up to playing either. It's too hot for me. Come on, I want to show you Mom's new project. It's over in the flower garden."

Anthony gratefully joined her. "Thanks for rescuing me. You guessed that I can't play tennis."

"You hid it well, but I had the feeling that was the reason."

"I can't play tennis. I can't play golf with your dad tomorrow. I can't ski. I don't even have a driver's license! Kay, I really don't belong in your group!"

"Will you stop this crap? It's no fucking big deal! Sorry about the language, but you're making me mad. Nobody really cares; we have lots of friends who can't play one sport or another. You are a great athlete, and you'll learn soon enough. Some of Dad's friends are so uncoordinated that it is painful to watch, but more power to them, they try. Your sport happens to be wrestling, and excuse me for mentioning that you're not too bad at it, Mister National Champion. And didn't you tell me you like to swim?"

"Yeah, I was involved in swimming before I started wrestling."

"Good, then let's put an end to this tennis complex of yours."

Kay's mother's project turned out to be nothing special, and the two of them walked around the grounds for a while. Kay held Anthony's hand firmly in hers. They walked along silently for a while, until Anthony asked, "How did you know I was embarrassed back there because I can't play tennis?"

"Call it a woman's intuition, but really it's because I love you, and when you hurt, I hurt. It makes me so sad when you are unhappy like that. This is our big weekend, and you're not here to feel bad. Anthony, I'm so excited that you're here, I could scream."

"I got news for you; you got competition. I really like your old man; he is one great guy."

"You really mean that, don't you?"

"Yes, I have to tell you I was a little afraid at first. You know he's a big deal, and I wasn't sure how he would accept me. He does not seem to care one bit where I come from and what happened in the past and that I'm only a college freshman. He talks to me like it is worthwhile to talk to me. He listens to me, and I think he respects my opinion."

"I just knew you'd like him. But to hear you say it and the way you describe it makes me glow all over. Now you know why I'm Daddy's girl. No matter what, he always made me feel like I was the most important person in the world."

By the time the two of them got back to the tennis court, everybody had worked up quite a sweat, and Kay took this opportunity to turn things in Anthony's favor.

"How about we all get into our bathing suits and head for the pool? Looks like all of you can use a refreshing dip." Everybody agreed, and half an hour later, they all gathered at the pool.

Kay's cousin looked like a million dollars in her skimpy little bikini, and when Kay's father saw her, he said to her dad, "You better hire a bodyguard for her or keep her locked up someplace." However, the hot-looking young dish was not the only good-looking female there. Kay's mother looked like she could still compete in the Miss New Jersey contest, and her sister might not have been the runner-up, but she was not far behind.

Kay, with her mile-long legs, looked pretty nice in her one-piece racing suit. But she was the least curvy of the women, and probably not the one to get whistled at on the beach. But no matter, she was still the best looking in Anthony's eyes. Kay might have called for this swimming party to give Anthony a chance to fully participate, but she also got to show him off. In a bathing suit he was one hell of an impressive man. His well-cut wrestler's body did not have an ounce of fat on it, and his slim waist made his broad shoulders look even wider. Kay's aunt and her daughter could not keep their eyes off him. This pleased Kay's mom, who could not wait to lord it over her sister.

True to form, Kay's dad expressed his admiration with a friendly comment. "Anthony, I would love to say that when I was a few years younger, I looked like you, but I would be lying. I must say you wrestlers do keep in shape. You probably have to spend more time in the training room than the football or basketball players, not to mention the baseball jocks, to which group I belonged."

Anthony had no idea that Kay's dad had played baseball. "You played baseball in college, sir?"

"I sure did. I was the ace pitcher my junior and senior year, even played Class D ball for half a season."

"What made you quit?"

"Not good enough. I had one pitch, a fastball, and once the batters got used to it, I was washed up. Bye, bye, baby. Go try your luck in business school."

Everybody except Kay's mother and aunt got into the pool. There was a lot of splashing around until Kay dared the others to a race. She was built for swimming, and with her water polo training, she knew she was the fastest. First, she handily beat her father and her uncle. Next, she took on her cousins, who also could not keep up with her.

Finally, it was Anthony's turn, and she called out, laughing, "You don't have to be a gentleman and let me win, 'cause I'm faster."

Anthony laughed back at her. "We'll see about that!" Kay underestimated Anthony's ability. She had to go all out to beat him. It was very close, but she did win, even though he had tried his best. Anthony did not mind that he lost. He quickly proclaimed Kay, "the Fourth of July Swim Champion."

XIX

The guests for Kay's mother's annual Fourth of July dinner started arriving at six o'clock in the evening. Kay had warned Anthony that the affair would be quite formal, and he had packed his best suit for the event. It was a pretty warm evening, so before dinner, drinks were served in the gazebo, which had been decorated for the occasion. The dinner was served in the formal dining room. The table looked magnificent. Most of the guests were familiar with the beautiful table settings, which featured handcrafted crystal that Kay's mother had specially made by a Czech craftsman. But it was the centerpiece that was always the big surprise. This time the centerpiece was smaller than at previous dinners, but spread down the center of the long table were perfectly matching smaller versions of the main centerpiece. The guests gave Kay's mother a nice round of applause. She had really outdone herself this time.

Kay was sitting next to her dad, and Anthony was at her side. Across the table from them was Henry

Gilman, CEO of a major Wall Street investment firm and frequent golf partner of Kay's father. Henry was engaged in an animated conversation with his table partner when he turned to Anthony.

"So you are the fellow who had all that adult action at a pretty young age?"

Kay's father stopped him short. "Henry, you are way out of line. Drop the subject right now!"

Henry would not let it go. "Why? He doesn't mind. You know as well as I do that Asians think differently about such things than we do, especially about sex. To him it must have been a big conquest."

Frank, Kay's father, stood up, his face flushed with anger.

"Henry, stop it, and get out of my house right now!" Henry looked surprised but did not get up.

"So now we have turned into a bunch of China lovers, have we? Oh, excuse me, he is supposed to be Filipino, like that makes a difference."

Frank was ready to explode, but he controlled himself as he repeated, "Get out of my house right now. Now! Or I'll throw you out!" It was not an idle threat. Frank was six foot four, and Henry was barely five feet eight. Henry turned to his wife.

"Come on, Betty, let's get the hell out of this place." On his way out, he could not resist taking a final jab at Kay. "Good luck with your Asian friend. Too bad you could not get a nice white boy." Frank took several steps in Henry's direction, but Henry quickly headed for the door. Kay got up slowly and raised her glass in her father's direction.

"Thank you, Daddy. Now I know why you have always been my hero." Someone started clapping, and spontaneously, the whole table joined in.

Kay's uncle raised his glass. "Thank you for letting my kids know that in this family, we don't tolerate bigots."

Frank turned to Anthony.

"Anthony, I'm sorry this had to happen, but for the record, I'm proud to have you date my daughter."

Anthony wanted to get up and thank Kay's father for those kind words, but Kay put her hand on his shoulder and in a soft voice said, "It's over. Let it rest." Then, in a much louder voice, she urged everybody to relax and get back to enjoying the dinner her mom had worked so hard on.

After dinner Kay's mother went over to her husband and gave him a big kiss. He tried to apologize for spoiling her big dinner, but she hushed him up.

"You did no more than to prove to me once again why I married you. I would have been very disappointed if you would have let that bastard get away with those stupid remarks."

Anthony approached the two of them. He stuck out his hand to Kay's dad, and said no more than, "Thank you." Then he leaned over to Kay's mom and gave her a gentle kiss on the cheek. "Thank you both for making me so very welcome in your house. Now I know why you have such a great daughter."

For the rest of the evening, Anthony and Kay were the center of attention. They were continually surrounded by the guests who asked a million questions about Princeton and how the two of them had met. As if they had previously agreed upon it, they both had the same story. They met in the library, and after a long talk, agreed to meet again for coffee. No need to mention Kay's roommate, Sue-Ellen. When the last guest had finally left, Kay suggested that before they turned in for the night, they could take a walk around the grounds. When they reached the pool and stood looking at the little waterfall in the shallow end, Kay turned to Anthony.

"Just because we're at my parent's house, that doesn't mean you can't kiss me. Would you please stop being so uptight about being here and kiss me?" She did not wait for Anthony to respond, but threw her arms around his neck and kissed him. After a while he took her hand and led her to the bench at the far end of the pool.

When they sat down, he said, "What your father did was pretty amazing. But I feel bad that it disturbed the dinner because of me."

Kay snuggled into his arms and tried to explain. "To Dad that was a perfectly natural thing to do. You must understand my family. My mom's mother was Catholic, and her father was an atheist. My Dad is Jewish, and he grew up in a poor neighborhood of mixed races and religions. There were first-generation Italians, Poles, Russians, Puerto Ricans, Africans, you name it. My dad grew up surrounded by that diverse group. He still keeps in contact with his best friend from high school, a black man from Nigeria. As a matter of fact, he is putting the man's three kids through college. I call the man my Uncle Josef.

"My first lesson on how my family felt came when I was in the second grade. For my birthday party, I invited a group of girls from my class. I didn't invite, Valerie, the little black girl who had quite recently moved into our neighborhood. I did not skip her on purpose; I just did not know the girl, and no one really played with her. My parents were not okay with that. They told me in no uncertain terms that that was very unfriendly and no way to treat a new girl in town, especially a girl who had not made any friends in her new school.

"I invited her the next day, and Mom gave me a note for her mother. The note read, 'We would love to have your daughter join us for Kay's birthday party. I have printed our address below. When you drop her off, please come in and introduce yourself. I would like to meet you, and I am sorry I have not had a chance to invite you sooner.' Mom and that lady are still good friends. I did not get to read the note until much later. For my sixteenth birthday, I got a wonderful gift from the girl's parents. Enclosed was a copy of the note with the inscription on the bottom. It read, 'The invitation to your birthday changed our daughter's life, and your parents have been our lifeline to this community.' I still tear up when I think about it."

As she said that, Kay crawled deeper into Anthony's arms.

After she had kissed Anthony good night at the guesthouse, Kay went back into the house, only to find her father still up. "I didn't expect to find you still up and about."

"Yeah, I wanted to finish some magazine articles I started a couple of days ago."

"Well, if you are up anyway, I wanted to ask you something. Did you really mean it when you said you are proud that Anthony and I are dating? What do you really think?"

"Kitten, you know I want nothing but the best for you, but with Anthony you are reaching very high."

"I know, Daddy, but he loves me, and I am beyond crazy about him."

"From seeing the two of you together, I agree, he loves you, and you have definitely hit a home run with that guy. Money might be the one big handicap in your relationship. The usual situation is that the guy is after the girl's money, but with Anthony it could scare him off. He is uneasy with what he sees here."

"You're right. At times he feels a little out of place here. But I love him enough to put up with that, and I know I can make him love me more than he fears our money."

XX

On the drive back to Princeton, Kay was silent. Anthony, who was not too talkative himself, asked her what was wrong.

"It's more than a month till school starts, and we won't be together for all that time. These last couple of days have been so great. But now it's over, and you'll be back at Princeton."

"A month is not forever. It will be over before you know it; and we do have a telephone. I'll call you often."

"I know, but I'll miss you a lot. Would you mind very much if I drive over some weekend?"

"Of course not! The cafeteria is never open on Sunday, and I'm free all day."

"That's a date. Don't be surprised if you see me appear every Sunday."

"You don't hear me object, do you?"

Their sophomore year was filled with athletics. Anthony won a basket full of wrestling medals, and Kay was named co-captain of the volleyball team, which was quite an honor for a sophomore. Besides her standout performances on the volleyball court, Kay was also promoted to first string on the water polo team.

During his freshman year, Anthony had repeatedly tried to contact Rita. Their lawyer had managed to have the judge's ruling set aside that Rita was not to have any contact with Anthony until he was twenty-one. Since he was considered an adult now, and no longer a ward of the state, Anthony could contact her at his discretion. But to his regret, Rita rejected any contact. The message he repeatedly received was, "It's still too early." Finally Rita gave in and agreed to talk to him by phone. Anthony's hands were trembling when he took up the phone.

"Hello, Rita, I've wanted to talk to you for a long time. How are you? How do they treat you?" Rita's response was calm and measured.

"I would prefer that you call me Aunt Rita. I really hope you are more comfortable with that." That took the wind out of Anthony.

"Rita, I mean Aunt Rita, I'm so sorry about what happened. I should never have; I promise I'll make it up to you."

Rita cut him short. "Anthony, you have nothing to apologize for. You owe me nothing. I should apologize to you. What happened was entirely my fault. As your guardian, I should not have had that type of relationship with you. I promised your mother to love you, not to make love to you. I am deeply ashamed of what I did, and I pray she can forgive me."

Anthony was silent on his end, and Rita continued. "Actually, they treat me better than I expected. It's jail, so I'm not free to go as I please, but I get to exercise a lot. They assigned me to what they call the beauty parlor. I get to wash the girls' hair and do their nails. I'm taking lessons, and soon I'll be able to cut their hair. When I leave here, they will actually give me a diploma. I'll finally officially be a beautician."

No matter how optimistic Rita tried to sound, Anthony still felt horrible that she was in jail and he was totally free. It kept on bothering him that what they did, they did together, and he had been a more-than-willing partner. He tried to explain this to Rita, but she kept steering him away from his part in their relationship. She tried to convince him that she and she alone should have controlled the situation.

"Anthony, listen to me. You might have thought at the time that you were all grown up, but really, you were still a confused kid looking for someone to love you. You were very vulnerable, and I should have been aware of it. The law was pretty tough on me, but not all wrong. I loved you like the son I never had, and I still do, but I should not have tried to make you into the husband I never had. I should have been aware that it was not normal that you never dated; you never even had a best friend. I wanted you all to myself and did not want to share you with anybody. I was very selfish. I'm paying for it, and I'm at peace with that. What still deeply troubles me is what I did to you and how it affects you."

Anthony listened carefully to what Rita said, but he still kept arguing that she never forced him to do anything he did not want to do.

"God help me, no," she said. "If I had forced you into things, I should not be here. Then I should be somewhere in a penitentiary put away for life. Anthony, like it or not, you were not an equal partner. Both of us might have been lost souls, but I was the adult, and you were a young boy not capable of making the decision you think you made. You were the one who was taking the place for all those men who wined and dined me but dropped me when I went to jail. I reveled in all the attention you paid me and in your fierce loyalty, the same loyalty you had shown your mother.

"You and your mother lived in a little private world. After she passed away, it became our little world, just you and me. While here in jail, I have made the following decision. I still want to be your aunt, solely the aunt who loves you very much, but absolutely no more than that. To make you understand that and to help you feel the same way about me, I will only have limited telephone contact with you and then only to find out if you are okay. You can absolutely not come here to see me in person. I will not agree to see you for at least another year and then only when you can introduce me to a girlfriend. Not just any old girlfriend. It has to be the girl you are in love with and hope to marry. Only then can I be sure that I have not harmed you for life, and that you can accept me as your aunt and no more than that."

Anthony had little choice but to accept what Rita said. He realized that no matter what, she would not let him come to see her for at least a year.

After the telephone call, Anthony was depressed. Kay noticed he was not himself. She decided not to push him. She was sure he would share whatever was bothering him with her. When he called her a few evenings later to say good night, he sounded very depressed, and Kay became worried. The next afternoon she skipped classes and barged into Anthony's room.

"Okay, tell me what is wrong. I was up all stinking night worrying about you. I know something is wrong."

"Nothing, really. Certainly nothing for you to worry about."

"You still don't get it, do you? When you are hurting, I can feel it in my bones, and all I want to do is hug you and make it better."

"Fine. If you must know, I spoke to my Aunt Rita the other day."

"So?"

"Well, she is blaming herself for what we did and completely ignores my responsibility for what happened. I helped put her in jail, and I feel terrible about it. So, now you know! It's not your problem, and I would rather not discuss it."

"You're right. The fact that you and Rita made love is not my problem. I am not the least bit hung up about it. It's that it still bothers you that is my problem. I love you, and I can't stand to see you like this. I understand you don't like to discuss your feelings with other people, but I'm Kay, and I am not other people. We share our feelings, remember? Now tell me what she said that so upset you."

Kay walked over to where Anthony was sitting, sat next to him, and pulled his head against her chest. She held him tightly in her arms and repeated her question.

"Now tell me what happened, and why you keep blaming yourself." As she held him, she could feel Anthony relax a little and some of the tightness slip out of his back muscles.

"Thanks for coming. I did want to talk to you about it, but each time I'm confronted with that whole miserable affair, I'm afraid of losing you."

"That, my dear, is less likely than getting hit by a meteorite. I'm here now, and everything is okay. We'll get through this together." Anthony sat up straight and started, as best he could, telling her what Rita had said. When he finished, they were both quiet for a while. Kay was the first to speak.

"I think the lady did some real soul-searching and now has a pretty clear picture of why it all happened. Mind you, I'm not condemning her, but the situation was ready for an accident to happen. You put a lady, with a hot body like Rita is rumored to have, and a well-built teenager with raging hormones together in a one-bedroom apartment with no privacy, and what do you expect to happen? Rita is not a bad person, but she should have allowed you to be more of a high school kid and carefully shielded her sexuality from you. But I guess she is human, and you're a hell of an attractive male. You gave her the love she was craving.

"You, on the other hand, did what every red-blooded American male would do. You responded to that hot body, which was offered to you on a platter. Did you have a chance to carefully think through the consequences? Of course not! Rita is right, she is not a criminal, but it was up to her to control the situation. As for your big fear, what do I think about what happened? Let me paint you a picture. You are this popular high school jock who has a steady girlfriend. The two of you have been dating all through high school, but when you left for different colleges, you drifted apart. I start dating you and later find out that you slept with your girlfriend in high school. Does that upset me? Of course not. The percentage of high school kids who are sexually active would have made me presume that you might have had sex with her.

"Now, before you come back at me and ask me what I would have done, would I have let you go all the way with me while we were dating in high school? Probably not, but who am I to say that? As I told you, I never really dated in high school, let alone had a steady boyfriend. So I can't really tell what I would have done if I were madly in love with a boy. But whether you like it or not, society has different standards for girls and boys and also for adults versus minors. Now, about our situation, do I think about you having sex with Rita? Not really. Except, of course, when it comes up in a conversation like we are having now. Do I blame you for what happened? No, what happened would happen to any young guy in that situation. To me, it's no bigger deal than if you had slept with your high school sweetheart."

When Kay finished her long oration, Anthony looked at her, and a smile started to appear on his face.

"Where did you come from? Did God send you? Why do I deserve to even know you?"

Kay squeezed him even tighter in her arms. "What I need is for you to hug me back and tell me that you're all right and that from now on, we share everything—the good, the bad, and even the terrible. Don't ever lock me out again!"

XXI

By the time Anthony and Kay entered their junior year at Princeton, it was an established fact that the two of them were an item. True to her word, Kay had taught Anthony how to play tennis. He still needed some work on his backhand, but he had developed a wicked serve and could hold his own in a friendly weekend game. Golf, however, was a different matter. Kay's father had started him on the game, but soon handed him over to the golf pro at the country club. Anthony showed some promise, but he could only take lessons during the times he visited in Deal. There was so much time between lessons that his progress was negligible.

Sue-Ellen left Princeton at the end of her sophomore year. Rather than stay in the dorms, Kay took an off-campus apartment with a friend from the volleyball team. Since Princeton allowed juniors to have a car at school, Kay brought hers up from Deal. She did not bring the Mustang, which she considered too flashy; instead, she brought a rather ordinary-looking

Chevy sedan. Her father had helped select the car for her, and as to be expected, the only thing ordinary was the outside appearance. He ordered every electronic accessory available and had a powerful aftermarket sound system installed. Kay did not really want any of those things, but since he was having fun, she let him have his way. Having her car at school allowed Anthony and her to visit with her parents on weekends when he was not involved in wrestling and she was not competing in one of her sports.

Sue-Ellen was not the only one to leave at the end of their sophomore year. Princeton had a very successful basketball season, and the team even made it to the NCAA tournament in March. They did not make the Sweet Sixteen, but Jamal received a lot of attention. When he told Anthony he intended to enter the draft and not return for his junior year, Anthony questioned the wisdom of not first completing his education. Jamal was quite sure of his decision.

"I don't underestimate the value of a Princeton education, and normally that would be the better choice, but for a guy like me, there is only one choice, and that is to go pro. They say I'll be in the top five in the draft, and that means a huge signing bonus and a great long-term contract. Just think, suddenly I'll have millions. I can move my family out of the hood to a nice suburban neighborhood. My younger sisters and brothers can go to really good schools, and my mom and dad can finally quit the jobs they hate. Just think of it, Anthony, I can move my family from the bottom to the very top of the middle class. We'll be poor no more. I've been dreaming about this ever since I started playing hoops on the public playground. If I wait two years, I could get injured, and who is to say I'll have another year like this? Next year I could disappoint. I would have missed the chance to do something really big for my family."

Anthony had to agree with his friend. "I understand, but I hate to see you go. I'll miss you terribly."

Jamal gave Anthony a big hug "I'll miss you too bro. You're the best friend I ever had." When school started the following September, Anthony moved into a single room in the same dormitory.

In the summer between his junior and senior year, Anthony once again stayed in Princeton. This time he got a job as a waiter at a popular downtown restaurant. Many of the local storekeepers and other local businessmen frequently had lunch at this restaurant, and Anthony got to know most of them quite well. They recognized him. Many of them had heard about his wrestling success and asked to be seated at a table served by Anthony. The wages were good, and the tips were always generous. Even the dinner crowd, which consisted mainly of tourists, tipped well, and by the end of summer, Anthony had saved up a nice amount of money.

XXII

The girl who shared the apartment with Kay did not return to Princeton for her senior year. Her father had suddenly passed away, and she decided to enroll in a school closer to home so she could be with her mother. A week after classes started in September, Kay asked Anthony to come to her apartment; she had something important to discuss. When Anthony arrived, she got straight to the point.

"I want you to move in with me."

"You only have a one-bedroom apartment; you want me to sleep on the couch again?"

"Stop that; it's not funny. I would never make you sleep on a couch, unless of course we slept there together. I'm asking you to move into the bedroom with me."

"That's a big step that will lead to other things."

"I am fully aware of that, and yes, I want to sleep with you. We make out a lot, but you always hold back. Now I want us to make love in a real way. I've been taking that damn contraceptive pill for a long time, hoping you would make love to me."

Anthony was a little flustered by this turn of events. "Are you sure we're ready for this?"

"You know I've been in love with you ever since you took me to the wrestling dinner. I know you love me. Yes, I'm sure we are ready."

"When do you want me to move in?"

"Now! We have waited long enough." Kay went to Anthony, took his hand, and pulled him into the bedroom. Anthony did not really resist, but he was hesitant. In the bedroom Kay started unbuttoning his shirt, and he made a vague move to stop her.

"Kay, I'm scared."

She smiled at him. "I know, darling, so am I. It's my first time, and look, I'm trembling a little. But I love you so much that I know it's okay. I know why you're scared. That's why I never pushed you, but this time the world will agree that it is okay."

Anthony teared up. He took Kay in his arms and carried her to the bed, where they helped each other get undressed. For a moment they awkwardly stood next to each other, but then Kay resolutely laid down, and pulled Anthony on top of her. He hugged and kissed her for a long while. When he finally entered her, she put her long legs around him and held him tight. Tears of joy were streaming down her face.

"Anthony, I love you so. I have waited forever for this moment." Anthony pressed his mouth to her ear and said very softly, "Kay, are we forever?"

"Yes, my darling, forever and then some."

They were both exhausted from the emotion and slept late the following day. When they woke up, they were still locked in each other's arms. It was Saturday, and they were in no hurry to get up and stop their hugging and kissing. Finally Anthony sat up.

"Kay, I should have asked this a lot earlier." As he said it, he rolled out of bed and got on his knees. "Kay, will you marry me?"

"Of course, darling! Yes, I'll marry you. Oh, Anthony, this is so great." She jumped right on top of him, and the two of them rolled around the floor like two little kids. Anthony hit the floor with the palm of his hand as if he were surrendering in a wrestling match.

"We have a problem."

"Impossible. How can we have a problem on the greatest day of my life?"

"I don't have a ring to give you."

"I don't need a ring. I have you, and that is all that counts."

"No, seriously, I have a solution. Get dressed. We have to go into town."

"Why? I said I don't need a ring, and I would much rather stay here and cuddle with you."

"I promise we'll have a lifetime of cuddling, but now I would like you to come with me."

After a quick breakfast, the two of them went downtown. Anthony headed straight for the bank.

"Why the bank? You're not getting money for a ring, are you?"

"No, I have a safe deposit box in which I keep all my valuable papers like my birth certificate. I also have something special in there." When Anthony opened his safe deposit box, he pushed aside a stack of papers and pulled out an oval, satin-covered red box. He opened the box and took out a brooch and handed it to Kay. Kay could not believe her eyes.

"Anthony, this is gorgeous. It's the most beautiful brooch I have ever seen. Where on earth did you get something so beautiful?"

"It was my mother's. My dad gave it to her to celebrate my birth. It's the one thing she steadfastly refused to sell, no matter how badly we needed the money. I think we can take some stones from it and make a nice engagement ring for you."

"Don't you dare! It was your mother's, and it's incredibly beautiful. We are in no way going to break it up."

"But we need a stone for your ring. My mother would be glad to know that your engagement ring was made out of stones from her brooch."

"No way, you can't do that! It was your mother's, and she got it from your father when you were born. Just holding it gives me the chills."

"Okay, but then I want you to have it as my engagement gift."

"Anthony, that is very sweet of you, and I do appreciate what you are offering me, but I can't take it. It's your link to your parents, and you must keep it."

"But I really want you to have it!"

"We could both own it as a couple. I'll wear it in their memory and as a symbol of our love for each other." As she said it, Kay burst out in tears.

"Kay, what happened? What is wrong?"

"Nothing is wrong. It's great. You have just let me into the one part of your life that you kept from me and never discussed. Sorry I'm so sentimental, but to me that means a great deal."

When they returned to the apartment, Kay called her parents. "Hi, Mom, stay on the phone, but ask Dad to pick up too. I have great news." When her father joined them on the line, she continued. "Mom, Dad, I'm engaged! Anthony asked me to marry him, and guess what, I said yes."

Both her parents were overjoyed. They insisted that the two of them drive up the next day, Sunday, so they could celebrate together. Anthony agreed, and they promised to come to Deal the next day. But Kay could not wait; she had to tell them about the brooch.

"We have this brooch. It was his mother's, and now we will own it together. It's so beautiful; I can't wait for you to see it. His father gave it to his mother when he was born. Just think, I'll be wearing it tomorrow." Kay had hardly finished her sentence when she burst out in tears again.

Her mother understood, and said very softly so only Kay and her husband could hear, "The last doubts have been washed away; now they are the perfect couple."

When they hung up the phone, Kay's father wanted to know what she meant by that.

"We're not all as prudish as you," she said. "I know that if my daughter loves a guy as madly as Kay loves Anthony, and she doesn't sleep with him for almost three years since they have been going together, there has to be some hang-up."

"You mean they are sleeping together now?"

"I should hope so. The boy's past has finally been buried, and he is hers now."

Kay's father seemed a little shocked. "So you really think they are sleeping together?"

"Get used to it, Frank. She is no longer a little girl. She is a grown woman who is bringing us the best future son-in-law we could hope for. I know you're crazy about that boy. And come to think of it, as soon as we were engaged, you could not wait to get me in bed. I was just about the same age Kay is now when we started rolling in the hay. Don't worry, I have not regretted it for one minute. As a matter of fact, I want you to come upstairs with me."

"Right now?"

"Yes, right now. It's the best offer an old fart like you is going to get today."

"Old fart? I'll show you an old fart," he said as he raced her upstairs to their bedroom.

XXIII

Anthony kept obsessing about getting Kay an engagement ring. Her mother was planning a huge engagement party at their country club, and he wanted her to have a ring at the party. Kay's father had warned him on that Sunday when they first came to show the brooch that it would be difficult to get her to wear a ring.

"She never wears any of the jewelry I have given her. I've tried earrings, bracelets, rings, you name it. She'll wear them once, and then they disappear in a large jewelry box in her room. She especially dislikes her mother's rings. She finds those big diamonds that are set way up from the setting too gaudy."

To get some advice, Anthony went to see Mr. Bradley, who owned the jewelry store two blocks down from the restaurant where he had worked during the summer. Mr. Bradley ate lunch at that restaurant almost every day, and he immediately recognized Anthony. Anthony explained the problem to Mr.

Bradley and hastened to add that he had a limited budget.

"I think I have the perfect ring for you. It's made by a young artist in Arizona, and I like his stuff so much that I bought his entire collection."

Mr. Bradley went into his office to get the ring. On top of a gold setting was a rectangular piece of jade with the long sides facing front and back. The surface was rounded, and in the middle were two diamonds set deep into the jade. Anthony tried to identify the color of the jade; it was greenish gray, much lighter than the dark green he normally associated with jade. There were some faint red and black streaks running through it. Anthony liked it a lot, but when he saw the price tag, it was above his budget. Mr. Bradley saw him look at the price tag.

"Don't worry, that is the list price. It is not the price for my local friends. The important thing is, do you like it, and do you think she will like it?"

"I like it a lot. It doesn't have the high set diamonds she hates."

"I'm sure we can stay within your budget. Give me a moment." Mr. Bradley went back into his office, presumably to look up his cost price. When he came back, he announced, "I made a nice friend's price, and I'll subtract an extra ten percent because you are a working student." With that he handed Anthony a piece of paper with the price. Anthony was happily surprised to see the big difference between the list price and the price Mr. Bradley was offering him.

"Really, you will let me have it for that?"

"That's your price."

"That's unbelievable. Thank you so much. That is really great of you. I can't thank you enough."

"As you can see, it pays to be a friendly waiter and a great wrestler for our university. I have seen you and your gal around town. You make a great couple."

Kay went wild when she saw the ring. "Oh my God, oh my God. It's perfect. However did you know I do not like the stand-up setting on a ring?"

"A little birdie told me. You never wear rings. Will you wear this one?"

"Are you kidding? It's never coming off my finger. Anthony darling, you are truly amazing. We have to go back to Deal this coming weekend. I'm dying to show my folks what you got for me."

Kay beamed as she proudly showed off her ring to her parents. Her mother thought it was the perfect ring for Kay.

"Honey, it's so you. Anthony, it's the perfect choice. You really do know our girl's taste." Anthony looked at Kay's father, but Frank just smiled back at him, and Anthony decided not to explain how he found out about Kay's dislike for certain types of rings. Kay's mother continued, "Now, you kids must allow me to arrange an engagement party. Don't worry, I won't do it during school. I'll arrange it during your Christmas vacation."

During the drive back to Princeton, Kay said, "Now we finally can go see Aunt Rita."

"We?"

"Anthony, you must stop thinking about yourself as *I*. From now on, it's going to be *we* in everything, and yes, I'm coming with you to see her. We must never forget that after the biggest loss of your life, she took you in. There was nobody else for you to turn to, and without her love, you might not have come through as well as you did. Sure, she made a big mistake, but she is human. And for me, she is the person who rescued the guy I love, and I love her! You're going to call her this coming week, and we are going to see our Aunt Rita."

"You never cease to amaze me. Coming from anyone else, I would say they were full of shit, but from you it really comes from your heart, doesn't it?"

"Buddy, like it or not, I am now part of your life. I love you so much that I want to be part of you, part of everything you do and feel. And I hope you feel the same way about me."

"I think I love you more."

"No, you don't. I love you more."

"No, you don't. I love you more."

"Impossible, I love you more." They kept up the banter for a while until Anthony said, "Can we stop someplace so we can make out?"

"I thought you'd never ask. I have not had a hug or a kiss since we left for Deal this morning, and I'm having withdrawal symptoms."

The very next day Anthony called Rita to tell her they were planning a visit. He also told her that he was engaged and that his fiancée would come with him.

"Engaged! Honey, that is the greatest news I have ever had. Anthony, that is fantastic! Where did you meet, how long have you known her, and what is her name? Tell me all about her. I'm so excited." She asked so many questions at once that Anthony did not know where to begin. He finally decided to start by telling the story of a chance meeting in the library. He tried to summarize their relationship the best he could, but it still became a long story.

By the time he finished, Rita had even more questions, followed by a slight rebuke. "You could have told me earlier that you were serious about this girl."

"I know, and I am sorry I didn't. I didn't try to hold it from you, but our telephone calls were short and a little impersonal. Besides, I had no idea how you would react. To be truthful I was afraid to tell you."

"Anthony, I'm your aunt and no more than that. I thought we were clear on that."

"Aunt Rita, a thousand times yes on that. Your reaction to my announcement is the best engagement present you could have given us."

"I'm so looking forward to meeting your girl. You said her name is Kay?"

"Yes, and she very much wants to meet you. The last time we spoke, you told me you would get your release date pretty soon. Did you get it?"

"Yes, I'll be released a few months from now, to be exact on January fifteenth next year."

"They never considered a parole?"

"No, I spoiled that when I got into an argument with another inmate. She called me a child molester, and I slugged her. They made a big deal about it, and I was lucky not to be sent to a maximum-security prison."

"Any plans as to where you will be going after your release? Will you go back to New York?"

"Never!"

"So you have not made any plans?"

"Yes, I have. When I was booked, they asked me to list my immediate family, but that was a problem. I never told you, but my parents and younger brother were killed in a car accident when I was sixteen. They had driven to a nearby town to see me in my debut on the football cheerleading squad. It happened on their way back, and I did not hear about it until the team bus dropped us off at our high school. A sixteen wheeler swerved across the road and hit them head on. The three of them died instantly."

"Aunt Rita, you could have shared this with me. Why didn't you?"

"Anthony, you had enough burdens of your own. You certainly did not need to hear my sad story. Anyway, for the rest of my high school years, I went to live with my mother's cousin and her family. As soon as I graduated, I headed for New York to try my hand at modeling, and over the years I lost contact with my family. The prison authority dug up an address, and I received a letter from a cousin urging me to come back home and live with her until I got back on my feet. She had already left the house when I came to live with her parents, but she was like an older sister to me. She wrote that she was very sorry we had lost contact and that over the years, she had repeatedly tried to find me. She went on to say that her five kids had all left home by now, and I was more than welcome to stay with her and her husband. They have a big house, and there is plenty of room for me."

"Are you going?"

"Yes, I am looking forward to going back to that little town where nobody knows anything about me, except maybe that I was a high school cheerleader ages ago."

"Where is this little town?"

"It's Axel, Nebraska, and I'm sure you have never heard of it. But I will go home and start all over again, and God willing, he'll give me a clean slate."

"You'll still be my aunt, won't you?"

"You're damn right, I'll always be your aunt; I am not giving up the one good thing in my life! When are the two of you coming to see me?"

"We'll check our class schedules, and I'll call you to let you know."

Fourteen days later Anthony and Kay were on their way to see Rita. The ride up to the prison took more than four hours. When they made a short stop for gas and some coffee, Anthony had a surprise for Kay. "Next time I'll be able to share the driving."

"How is that? You don't have a license."

"I didn't tell you. It was supposed to be a surprise; last summer I took driver's lessons, and I plan to take my driver's test next week."

"Anthony, that is really great! It will make you feel better when you don't always have to be the passenger. Don't tell my dad. He'll go right out and buy you a car."

"That's crazy. He wouldn't, and he shouldn't."

"Don't bet on it. He loves me a lot, but you're a guy, and now he has the son he always wanted. Really, he's crazy about you. If we ever get into an argument, I know whose side he'll be on, and it's not mine." Anthony protested a little, but he had to admit that he knew her parents really liked him.

"I love being with them. They always make me feel like I belong. You are very lucky to have such great parents."

Kay laughed. "I know that, but I told you I would share."

They walked hand in hand back to the car, and when they got in, Anthony said, "Next time I'll be able to get in on the driver's side."

The reunion with Rita was very emotional but much easier than any of the three of them had expected. When Anthony and Kay entered the prison cafeteria, which served as the visiting room, Rita was sitting at one of the tables waiting for them. Even though she was wearing no makeup, and her long blond hair was pulled tightly back into a ponytail, you could still see she was a very good-looking woman who showed little signs of aging. She jumped up and ran to Anthony and gave him a big hug. She did not kiss him. Next she turned to Kay.

"Can I give you a hug too?" Kay stretched out her arms, and Rita gave her a big bear hug. "Kids, this is so great! You did not turn your backs on this old lady. Kay, just knowing that you even wanted to see me makes me cry. Look at you, so tall and slender. Anthony, she's beautiful!" Again she reached for both of them and embraced them. "This really makes me want to live again."

Anthony pulled back and looked Rita straight in the eye. "What does that mean?"

"Nothing, just a way of telling you how happy you have made me with this visit. Come sit down. We have a lot of time to make up, and I have a million questions." They sat down in the empty cafeteria. Rita could not stop talking. "Anthony, you look great, and Kay, I can't get over how beautiful you are. Now I fully understand why Anthony told me over the phone how much he loves you. You are truly a blessing."

For almost an hour, the three of them carried on an animated conversation—mostly serious, but there was also a lot to laugh about. As the visiting hour drew to a close, Anthony returned to Rita's remark about wanting to live again.

"Aunt Rita, that bothered me. What exactly did you mean by that?"

"You don't miss anything, do you? Okay, I might as well tell you. You'll find out eventually anyway. The real reason I never qualified for parole is that I tried to commit suicide a few months after I got here."

Kay burst out crying; she bounced up from her chair and took Rita in her arms. "You poor thing, there was nobody for you, and you did so much for Anthony when his mother died. You saved him. You gave me my Anthony, and I love you." She continued to hold Rita real tight. "Aunt Rita, you're my hero. Promise me that you will never try anything like that again."

Rita kissed Kay on the forehead. "You truly are a blessing. Anthony, you might have had to endure a lot as a child, especially losing your mother so early, but now you have received a very special gift. Take good care of her. She is the only person who has made me feel good about myself in a long time. I pray that one day I get to hold your baby, and then I'll truly know that God has forgiven me for my sin."

Kay was still holding on tightly, and Anthony wanted to respond, but at that moment, a guard entered the cafeteria to announce that visiting time was over. No ifs or buts about it, Kay and Anthony had to leave. They stretched their good-byes as long as they could, and Rita hung on to both of them until the guard stopped her at the door.

The trip back to Princeton seemed much longer than the trip up earlier that day. They drove along silently for most of the trip until Kay said, "We're going to keep her in the family."

"Of course. By the way, did I tell you that you are truly amazing and that I love you very much?"

"I love to hear it; you can't ever say it enough."

XXIV

Anthony came in late from wrestling practice and headed straight for the shower. Kay had dinner all ready, and she came into the bathroom to tell him to hurry. She watched him dry off his muscular body and offered to dry his back.

Stroking his muscular back, she asked, "Does it bother you that I have such small breasts? Don't you wish they were larger, and that I would have a little more flesh on my behind and hips?" Anthony turned around and started laughing. "Don't laugh at me, I'm serious. I want to know if it bothers you that I have such small breasts."

"Okay, I'm serious. You have the tall, slender figure that fashion models would die for. On your gorgeous body, big breasts would look ridiculous. Anyway, they are not that small. They just look small because you are tall and have wide shoulders. If you must know, I love your breasts. They are perfectly shaped and impish. I love them! Get over that misplaced complex about your figure. You're slender.

You're beautiful, and your long legs are very sexy. You must have noticed men looking at them. What brought on this conversation anyway?"

"Well, last night was the first time since we have been living together that we fell asleep without first making love."

"If you'll give me a rain check, we can make up for that right now."

"Okay, but after dinner; it's ready, and it's getting cold."

"To hell with dinner. Thinking about your breasts has gotten me all excited, and I want to get my hands on them right now."

Kay did not have to be persuaded. "You really know how to make me feel good, don't you?" She pulled off her clothes, and taunting Anthony with her naked body, she headed for the bedroom.

XXV

The parking valets at the country club could hardly find room for all the cars of the guests arriving for Kay and Anthony's engagement party. Kay's mother had gone all out. She had invited everybody she knew; even her most casual acquaintances got an invitation. The rest of the arrangements were equally over the top. Kay joked about it to Anthony.

"And I told you my father was ostentatious. Well, it looks like Mom is not shy about showing off either."

"That's not really fair. She is a lot prouder of you than you ever realized, and this is her way of showing how much she loves you. I take it as a huge compliment that she is doing this for our engagement. If she had just planned a reception at your house, that would have been fine. But a sit-down dinner for all these guests and three bands to entertain them is just beyond. I've been working on a speech I want to give to thank your parents, but I'm having trouble right now. It is too sentimental."

"Go ahead, be sentimental. Our relationship is very special, and I too can get very emotional about it. It's so thoughtful of you to want to thank them at the party; most guys would never even think of it."

Anthony and Kay circulated among the tables, making sure they got to speak to every guest. Kay's appearance was striking. People were not used to seeing her quite so glamorous. Before the Christmas vacation, her mother had taken her into New York to select a dress. In the store they had a small disagreement about a dress her mother wanted her to try on. Kay thought it was much too expensive and a little too fancy. But her mother insisted, and Kay tried it on. When Kay stepped out of the dressing room, her mother's face lit up.

"Honey, you look fabulous. There is no way we are not getting that dress." She turned to the saleslady. "You're sure it's one of a kind?"

"Yes, Mrs. Goodman. It's an original we just got in this past week." On the morning of the party, her mother insisted that Kay go with her to the beauty parlor, so the two of them could have their makeup and hair done together. Again, Kay resisted, but her mother would have none of it.

"Weeks ago I made this appointment for you, and I gave Edgar a picture of you, so he would know how to style your hair. Bear with me. I am having too much fun with all these arrangements to argue with you. When you were a little girl, you never let me dress you up. This is my last chance. Actually, that is not true. For your wedding you'll wear a spectacular gown. After that I promise to stop interfering with what you wear. Then I'll treat you like a grown woman and leave it to Anthony to help you decide what to wear."

Later that day, when Kay was dressed and came down the stairs, Anthony and her dad were almost speechless. Her mother was beaming.

"What do you men think of the way she looks?" Anthony had trouble expressing how beautiful she looked, but Frank had no trouble finding the right words.

Looking at his wife and daughter, he said, "I'm looking at the two most beautiful women in the world. One is my wife, and the other my daughter. What more could a man wish for?"

During the dinner, Kay's mother's friends repeatedly mentioned how beautiful Kay looked, and she often heard, "They make a beautiful couple. He's so handsome, and they look perfect together." Kay's mother was floating on air. When Kay was growing up, she had often heard remarks as to how skinny her daughter was and how she never had any boyfriends. The remarks hurt her much more than she admitted, but now she felt fully vindicated. Let them go ahead and brag about their children. Kay had topped them all!

When the dessert was being served, Anthony went over to the stage and took the microphone.

"If I can have your attention for a moment, I would like to say a few words to my fiancée, Kay, and her parents, Mr. and Mrs. Goodman. They don't want me to address them as Mister and Missus. They have repeatedly asked me to call them Mom and Dad. Since I have not had a mom and dad for a long time, I still have to get used to it. Kay has told me she will gladly share, and that she wants them to be my mom and dad too. So here goes. Kay, Mom, and Dad, I would like to tell these good people how I feel about you and why I am so proud to join your family. I entered Princeton during a very difficult time in my life, and the beginning was kind of rough. At one point I even thought about dropping out of school.

"But then I met an angel. She lifted me up and figuratively carried me up to the clouds. She washed away past hurt and made me feel good about myself. Then this angel took me home to meet her parents. Was I scared? You bet I was scared. My fears were misplaced. They welcomed me into their home and made me feel as if they were happy to have me. I soon learned that, like their daughter, the two of them don't pretend. When they say you're welcome, they mean it. During that wonderful first visit, there was an incident, and Dad stood up for me. It was like he placed me behind his broad shoulders and protected me from a blow I could not take. What he did made a deep impression on me. I admired the character he showed, and this admiration has only grown over the past three years. I have a deep respect for him, and I only hope I can live up to his high standards. I not only respect him, but I have also come to love him too.

"And then there is Mom, who came up to me and placed her hand on my shoulder. 'I'm so sorry,' she said, and kissed me on the cheek like a mother would kiss your scraped knee after you had fallen down. How could I help but love this woman? And my angel? Well, she is something very special. When we met, I had quite a few ghosts in my closet, but she chased them all away. When I think about how she brought me and my only relative back together, I still get tears in my eyes. Kay, you did a wonderful thing, and I want the folks here to know that you made my aunt's life a lot better. Angel, your goodness is not only written all over my life but hers too."

Anthony signaled a nearby waiter to hand him a glass of wine. He raised the glass.

"Please join me in a toast to the three most wonderful people in this world and to thank Mom and Dad for giving this great party in honor of Kay and me. I'm thrilled to have met all of you."

Everybody stood and clapped loudly. Here and there a handkerchief appeared to wipe away a tear. Kay and her parents came to the stage, and Kay and her mother gave Anthony a big kiss. Frank gave him a big bear hug. The guests cheered and kept clapping for a long time.

XXVI

Immediately upon their return to Princeton after their Christmas vacation and engagement party, Anthony and Kay started discussing Rita's upcoming release from jail. January 15 was rapidly approaching. Kay kept urging Anthony to make plans to be there for her release. But Anthony had a problem: the regional invitational wrestling tournament was scheduled for that week. And this year it would be held at Princeton.

"It will be very hard to explain to Coach that I won't be there."

"I realize that it is difficult, but I don't care." Kay was adamant. "We will not let her leave prison alone without anybody there to meet her. We just cannot have her walk out after three years to a waiting taxi, which will take her to the bus station for a twenty-hour-plus trip home. No matter what, we will be there when she comes through those doors!"

"I'll sit down with Coach and discuss it. He knows all about Rita, so I hope he'll understand."

Coach understood perfectly, and even though he hated to miss his star wrestler for this big tournament, he agreed this should take precedence.

They made arrangements to have Rita's clothes taken out of storage and packed into two brand-new suitcases, which they would pick up on the way to the prison. The only problem that remained was the release time; Rita would be released at 8:00 a.m. sharp. Anthony did not have a problem with that.

"We'll drive up the day before and stay overnight in a motel near the prison."

Promptly at eight the big door in the prison gate opened, and Rita was escorted to the sidewalk. The guards said good-bye to her and went back inside, leaving Rita standing alone. She was dressed in the same clothes she had worn when they booked her three years ago. She was clutching a paper bag with the few belongings they had returned to her. She looked scared as she searched for the taxi she thought the prison authorities had ordered for her. She did not notice the gray Chevy parked across the street until it made a sharp U-turn and stopped right in front of her. She could not believe what happened next. Anthony and Kay jumped out of the car and ran to embrace her.

"You're here! You are really here. Oh my darlings, I'm so scared. Thank God you're here. I prayed that maybe you'd come, but I dared not ask."

The three of them did not pretend to hold back the tears as they stood there tightly holding on to each other.

"Aunt Rita, we have another surprise. Let's get into the car, and we'll show you."

"I really don't deserve any more surprises. You have made me so glad! No one can imagine what it means to me to have the two of you here. For weeks I've dreaded getting out. I have not been outside that prison for three years, and I have no idea how to handle getting on the bus to go to Axel. You'll help me, won't you?"

"Okay, but first open this envelope." Rita opened the envelope and pulled out a plane ticket to Axel, Nebraska. The excitement was more than Rita could take; she broke down in heavy sobs. Kay put her arms around her, and Rita buried her head in her chest. When she recovered a little, Rita, with tears still streaming down her cheeks, tried to thank them.

"You two, you're just the best. This is incredible, that you would do this for me. The two of you being here when I got out was already the best gift you could have given me, and now this. How do I deserve you two? You're beyond great. I love you! I love you so much! Here, let me hug you again. Just hold me close for a while, so I can absorb what is happening. I'm afraid I'll wake up and find out that all this was a dream."

Anthony was the first to interrupt the magic bond between the three of them.

"Aunt Rita, we have to hurry, or you'll miss your plane. The airport is not too far, but we have to leave plenty of time for check-in and security." At the airport Rita was once again overwhelmed by another surprise. Anthony pulled the two new suitcases from the trunk of the car.

"We thought you might want your clothes back." Rita's screech of joy could be heard all the way through the airport garage. Next, Kay reached into the trunk and pulled out a nicely wrapped package.

"Our aunt will travel in style, so, Aunt Rita, we have selected a nice outfit for you to wear on the trip home. When we get into the terminal, please go into the ladies bathroom and put on your new outfit. I'll take your old clothes home and burn them, together with a lot of bad memories. Anthony and I will not have you arriving in Axel in the same clothes you wore when you entered prison."

Rita was speechless. Her hands were shaking when Kay handed her the package of clothes. All Rita could say was, "I was right. God did send you from heaven."

"No, he did not. We just love you, and being here makes us just as happy as it does you. To see you free and happy means the world to us."

"Now I truly know the two of you really love me," Rita said. Anthony put the suitcases down and came over to put his arm around Rita.

"Aunt Rita, there should never have been any doubt."

Surprises were not over for the day. When they entered the departure hall, a lady stood up and approached them.

"No, it can't be. It's my cousin Betty." Rita raced forward to meet her halfway. Anthony and Kay held back while the two women embraced.

"How on earth did you recognize me so quickly?" Betty asked. "It's been almost forty years since we saw each other."

"You haven't changed that much. Now you look very much like your mother did when I left for New York. Betty, I'm so sorry. I just took off for New York and never kept in contact. I should never have left home like that, but New York was such a magnet. I paid dearly for my foolishness."

"Hush, girl. Everything is okay now. We have you back, and I'm taking you home." Before Betty and Rita went through security, Rita said a tearful good-bye to Anthony and Kay. Even though it was hard for her to say good-bye to the two of them, she had too much to look forward to, to let the sadness of the moment take the upper hand.

During the drive back home, Kay said, "I'm emotionally drained. How do you feel?"

"I feel really good about a lot of things, and as usual, I was right."

"What on earth are you talking about?"

"I told the guests at our engagement dinner that you are an angel, and I was right."

"Well, if I am an angel, at least I have a heavenly partner." After they had stopped again for gas and a bite to eat, Kay said, "I can't wait to get back home."

"Why is that?"

Kay looked up from the wheel and gave Anthony a sly little smile.

"If you can't guess, I won't tell you."

XXVII

At the end of April, Anthony received an invitation to try out for the US Olympic Wrestling Team. His coach had expected it and discussed it with Anthony. But when the actual invitation arrived, Anthony was ecstatic. He read it over and over again. The trials for the US Olympic Wrestling Team would be held at the Carver Hawkeye Arena in Iowa City, Iowa, April 21–22.

Very early in the morning of April 20, Kay drove Anthony to Newark Airport, so he could catch the seven o'clock flight. He insisted she drop him off at curbside check-in, that there was no need for her to come in with him.

When he kissed her good-bye, she said, "I'm going to miss you!"

"It's not like I'll be gone for a long time. I'll be back in a few days. They'll probably send me home after the first few rounds."

"Sure, and all those medals and trophies we have at the apartment were store-bought." When Anthony headed for the entrance to the terminal, Kay called him back. "Hey, you, I need one more kiss." As if she had some premonition, she held on to him for a while and had trouble letting him go. "Call me as soon as you arrive."

Kay got back to Princeton in time for her morning classes. After class she walked over to Woodrow Wilson Café for lunch. She had just gotten her tray and was heading to a table when she glanced at a TV that was tuned to CNN. At that moment the program was interrupted with a news flash.

"CNN has now received additional information on Mohawk Airlines Flight 201, which went down earlier this morning near Davenport, Iowa."

Kay dropped the tray she was carrying and screamed, "No, it's not true. It can't be!" Her hands went up to her face as she fell to the floor. People seated in the café came running over to help. Kay was totally incoherent and kept calling out, "Anthony, Anthony. They got the wrong plane. It can't be his plane. It's not Anthony's plane."

Three students who knew Kay tried to pick her up and comfort her. By hearing her call out, "Anthony," they quickly figured out what had happened. Two of them took Kay between them and led her to the dispensary for some calming medication. At the dispensary she was administered a strong sedative. They tried to get her to lie down to let the sedative take effect, but Kay was inconsolable.

Her cell phone rang, and the nurse answered it for her.

"It's your father."

Kay grabbed the phone. "Daddy! Daddy, Anthony's plane went down."

Her father quickly interrupted her. "Anthony is alive. Wounded but alive."

"Oh, Daddy, really? Really?" Kay sat up. Her sobbing stopped. "How do you know? Are you sure?"

"Yes, we heard about the crash an hour ago, and my office immediately contacted the airline. My secretary managed to get them to tell her the name of the ambulance service that was on the scene. She called the company's dispatcher, and he told her Anthony survived the crash and was in one of their ambulances on the way to Genesis Medical Center in Davenport, Iowa."

"I have to go there. I have to see him."

"Yes, kitten, that has been arranged. My driver will pick you up at your apartment in less than an hour to take you to the airport. Throw a few things in a suitcase and be ready to leave when he gets there."

"Daddy, please come with me, please."

"I will. I am first going to Livingston to pick up my friend Dr. Levine. He is the chief surgeon of the Burn Center at Saint Barnabas Medical Center in Livingston. The reason I asked him to come with us is that we were told that Anthony's feet are badly burned. By the time I get to the airport, the company plane will be ready to take us out there. I already instructed the pilots to file a flight plan that will get us to Davenport as soon as possible."

"You're so great! Thank you, Daddy. You always know how to get things done. But is Anthony in danger?"

"The best information we can get is that his life is not in danger, but his feet are badly burned. That's why I want to get Dr. Levine out there as soon as possible. He's the best there is when it comes to burns." The sedatives had taken effect, and Kay was a lot calmer while she waited for her father's chauffeur to take her to the airport.

During the flight Kay could not sit still. When she was not walking up and down the cabin, she was trying to have Dr. Levine tell her Anthony would be all right.

"Without actually examining his burns, I cannot predict what we can do about his feet. But I can assure you we have never lost a burn patient who did not have seared lungs or damage to some other vital organ." That made Kay feel better, but she could not rest until she could see Anthony with her own eyes.

The pilots had called ahead, and a taxi was waiting to rush them to the hospital. Anthony was heavily sedated, and it did not really register who they were when they entered his room. After Dr. Levine had identified himself, the doctors allowed him to examine Anthony's feet in the sterile setting of one of the operating rooms. Dr. Levine was only gone for half an hour, but to Kay it seemed forever. When he finally came back into the room where Kay and her father had anxiously been waiting, he had good news.

"Both feet are badly burned, but I have seen worse. I am pretty sure we can save both his feet. But to do that, I need artificial skin to cover all the exposed areas, and they don't have that here. Frank, I have to get him back to Saint Barnabas, but it is too risky to take him back in your plane."

"I was afraid of that. So I asked my secretary to arrange a medical evacuation plane with one or two nurses. That plane should be here in the next hour or two."

Kay put her arms around her father's neck. "Daddy, you're just unbelievable!" Dr. Levine agreed with her.

XXVIII

The heavy doses of pain-killers were wearing off, and Anthony opened his eyes. "Where are we? Kay, how did you get here?"

"You are back in New Jersey. We brought you to Saint Barnabas Burn Center." It hardly registered.

"Kay, my legs, they hurt so bad." Kay tried to comfort him, taking care not to disturb the IV and the massive bandages covering his feet.

"I know, honey. I know it hurts. They'll be here in a few minutes to take you to the operating room. They say that will relieve some of the pain." Kay had not left Anthony's side since they were reunited in Davenport. She had insisted on flying with him on the medical evacuation flight and was still clutching his hand when they wheeled him into the emergency room at Saint Barnabas.

It wasn't till early the next morning that Anthony was brought back to his room from the recovery room. He was awake and lucid, but still in terrible pain. The hospital staff had made arrangements for Kay to stay the night, but she never laid down on the cot they had brought in for her. She just sat in the big chair, waiting for Anthony's return. Even though she had never been very religious, she felt a need to pray. Repeatedly, she thanked God for saving Anthony's life. She was so grateful that his life had been spared and that she did not lose him that she forgot to pray for his full recovery.

About every half hour, a nurse would come into the room to check on Anthony, and at nine o'clock, an intern came to see him. He entered the room with a copy of the morning newspaper tucked under his arm and greeted Anthony with, "How is our hero feeling this morning?"

Neither Anthony nor Kay had any idea what he meant by that, and Anthony just responded that he was still in terrible pain.

"I'll order some more morphine for you, but I just have to read you the *Times's* headlines." The headlines read, "College Student Rescues Mother and Child from Burning Wreckage of Mohawk Flight 201."

The story went on to describe how the plane had come down on its belly, but skidded head on into a building. The cockpit and most of the first-class passenger compartment were destroyed, and fire broke out in what was left of the front part of the plane. All the economy passengers managed to escape via the slide. The cabin crew urged the passengers to get away from the burning plane, but Anthony Walker, a senior at Princeton University, saw a woman in the window of the last row of first class, desperately waving for help. Somehow Anthony managed to climb back up the slide. He raced through the smoke-filled cabin and found the woman with both feet pinned under the seat in front of her. Her three-year-old son was clinging to her.

In an amazing feat of strength, he bent back the seat to free the woman. The seat had crushed both her legs, and the woman could not stand up. Anthony picked her up, took her and the child in his arms, and raced over the burning cabin floor to the slide. From the bottom of the slide, the cabin crew carried the woman and her child to safety, but Anthony was lying on the ground, both his sport shoes on fire. Another passenger raced over and put his jacket tightly around Anthony's feet in order to smother the flames. An ambulance transported Anthony to Genesis Medical Center in Davenport, Iowa, where it was determined that he had third-degree burns on both his feet. Anthony's fiancée's father, the well-known industrialist, Frank Goodman, had Anthony flown by a medical evacuation flight to Saint Barnabas Burn Center in New Jersey. At last report his condition was stable, but very serious.

The article went on to give the names of the two pilots, the first-class cabin stewardess, and the five first-class passengers who had been killed in the crash. The woman Anthony rescued was identified as Nancy Rutherford, wife of Nebraska Senator Mark Rutherford.

Kay was speechless. She squeezed Anthony's hand, which she had been holding, so tightly that he flinched.

But before she could say anything, Anthony said, "I am sorry, Kay. I didn't mean to get hurt. I didn't want to cause you any pain."

"There is no need to be sorry. You saved the woman's life! Anthony, you saved someone's life! Do you realize what you did? It's amazing. Darling, you saved her life and that of her child. It's incredible!"

The intern put down his newspaper. "Let me turn on the TV. You are all over the news. You are a national hero." Nowhere in the news was it mentioned that Anthony had been on his way to the Olympic tryouts and that his dream of representing the United States in the Olympics had been lost forever.

When Frank Goodman's car pulled up to the house, Sue ran out to meet him. She tried to kiss him, but he buried his head in her arms and burst into tears.

"We almost lost him. We almost lost Anthony."

Sue tried to comfort him. "You really love that boy, don't you? He is the son I could never give you, and I adore him too. Go ahead and cry. I've been crying all day."

Frank Goodman never cried in front of other people; Sue was the only one who had ever seen him cry. He was not known as an emotional man. He had a reputation for being tough, but always extremely fair. He could make hard decisions without being sentimental about it. But Sue Goodman knew better. She knew he was vulnerable, and she was always there to comfort him when he needed emotional support. They had met at a party in New York. She was a young model, and he was the whiz kid at an investment firm. The attraction was instant, and they had been married for almost thirty years. It was never clear who proposed to whom, and the joke between them was that they had proposed to each other.

When people first met Sue, they would take her for a trophy wife. Her good looks and ostentatious jewelry would give them the wrong impression. Once people got to know them as a couple, they realized how devoted they were to each other. It took a while for their emotions to subside, but then Sue took her husband by the hand and led him into the house.

"Quick, come on in. The TV is on. You will not believe what our Anthony did."

XXIX

Newspapers, television, and magazine reporters all wanted to interview Anthony, but Kay was a very strict gatekeeper. However, she could not keep everybody out. Five days after the crash, Senator Rutherford appeared at the hospital. He smiled when he learned that he needed Kay's clearance before he could see Anthony, but he understood completely. The senator greeted her in the downstairs hospital lobby.

"I have come to express my and my wife's gratitude to Anthony, but I also want you to know we understand what you had to go through. You could have lost your fiancé in the crash, and again when he heroically re-entered the plane to save my wife and son. Words can never describe the gratitude we feel for Anthony, but you too will be in our hearts forever."

Kay escorted the senator upstairs to Anthony's room. When the senator met Anthony, he became very emotional, and Anthony was embarrassed by all the superlatives he used to describe Anthony's actions.

"I don't know if you'll ever understand what you have come to mean to me. You saved my wife and son, my two most precious processions." Anthony assured the senator that anyone placed in his position would do the same thing. "We would hope so, but we both know that is not true. What you did is exceptional."

The senator told them his wife's legs were already healing nicely, and the doctors had assured her she would make a full recovery. He did say, however, that he had been advised to seek professional counseling for both his wife and young son to help prevent possible post-traumatic stress symptoms.

After Anthony had spent two weeks in the hospital, Kay started lobbying for permission to take him home. She assured the doctors that she could take care of the daily change of bandages and that she would be home to take care of him. She had already informed the university that she intended to skip at least one semester to stay with Anthony. Since Anthony would also be missing at least one semester, they would still graduate together. Once they were back in their apartment, they had a constant stream of visitors. The wrestling coach came by at least once a week, and Anthony's ex-teammates took turns visiting him.

The big surprise was a long letter from Sue-Ellen. In it she wrote how wrong she had been and how she hoped Anthony could forgive her for her stupid behavior. Addressing Kay, she wrote, "You were absolutely right. I behaved like a fool, and now hate myself for it. You were right all along, and now my loss is your gain. I truly wish you two all the best, and I have to admit that, whatever I said and did, I secretly still have one hell of a crush on Anthony."

Kay brushed all the excuses aside. She could never forgive Sue-Ellen. "That bitch. Now that you are a national hero, she wants to be your friend. Sure, and I am supposed to forget the despicable things she said? Never!"

Much more exciting was the visit from Jamal. He flew in from Seattle to find out for himself how Anthony was doing. He greeted Anthony in his old familiar style.

"You are one hell of a brave dude. I knew you were a gutsy guy, but to run back into a burning plane is just beyond." He did not hide the fact that he was worried about Anthony's condition, and he wanted to know how far the doctors thought he would recover. Anthony assured him that the prognosis was pretty good.

"I have lost the two small toes on my right foot, and I will have to have at least six more operations to get rid of some of the scar tissue, but the doctors assure me I'll be able to walk again normally."

Jamal was relieved. "Man, you had me worried. When I first heard you were in that plane, I could not get any more information about you other than the fact that you were wounded. It took forever before they released more information, and I finally found out you were in serious condition, but thank God, not critical. That's when I called Kay and got the full story. And by the way, you miserable creatures, you never told me you are engaged. Anthony, what took you so long? I told you she is the best there is. You might have a pair of burned feet, but you are still one hell of a lucky bastard."

Jamal's visit did wonders for Anthony's mood. The two of them sat up most of the night talking about old times and what they had been doing since Jamal left school. Anthony wanted to hear all about what life was like in the NBA and especially how Jamal's family was doing in Seattle. Jamal's return on campus caused quite a bit of excitement. The next day he made the rounds to say hello to his old teammates and coaches.

One visitor, Andrew Spencer, was not welcome after Kay discovered he was a reporter. The situation became worse when he asked Anthony, "You are the same Anthony Walker who was involved in the head-line stories about your guardian, aren't you?"

Kay, eyes blazing, bolted out of her chair. "Out, get out! How dare you. Get out." Andrew held up his hand as if to ward her off.

"I'm not here to talk about that, and in no way would I mention that in a story. Look, I'm on your side. Maybe you should let me explain."

Anthony wanted to know what Andrew had to say. "Kay, let's hear what he has to say, maybe he means well."

Andrew explained that he had objected to the way the newspapers had covered the story about Rita.

Because of his age, many of the newspapers did not mention Anthony's name in the story, and by the time his name did appear, Andrew had stopped following the story. He did not connect Anthony to his father, General Walker, until he read about Anthony's actions after the plane crash. He did some research and discovered that Anthony was also involved in the headline stories about Rita.

"Anthony, I was and am still prejudiced because I know all about your father. I have come here not so much to talk about you, but I want to tell you about your father. I don't know if you are aware of the fact that he too was involved in a plane crash. Unfortunately, it took his life. But it is important for you to know that he too was a hero."

Anthony admitted that he knew next to nothing about his father.

"Well, let me tell you, General Bruce Walker was a real war hero. He was a young first lieutenant when, during combat, his platoon got scattered during an enemy ambush. When his unit retreated behind friendly lines, three of his men were missing. By himself he went back behind enemy lines to search for his men. When he came upon them, two were seriously wounded, and the third was furiously trying to hold off a group of enemy soldiers closing in on them. Without regard for his own safety, Lieutenant Walker charged the enemy position. He got hit twice, but he charged on and managed to kill the advancing enemy soldiers, seven in total. He and the soldier who was not wounded managed to carry the two wounded ones back to their unit."

Anthony had never heard any of this and wanted to know how Andrew knew. Andrew looked at him. "I have firsthand knowledge of what happened."

"How is that?"

"One of the wounded soldiers your father brought to safety was my father, Private First Class Spencer. He would not have survived had it not been for your father's heroic actions. I am surprised you never were told any of this; your father received the Medal of Honor for his actions. Being a hero must be in your DNA."

Anthony had a million questions. His mother had never told him anything about it, and he assumed his father had never told her. Kay was excited to hear about Anthony's father.

"Anthony, I would have loved to have known your father. He must have been a wonderful man. Now that I hear what he did, I see that you are so much like him."

Andrew Spencer wanted to know if Anthony had any objections to his writing a story about his father and the similarities between the actions of father and son. Anthony did not like the idea, but Kay did.

"Why not, Anthony? Your father's actions deserve to be retold. You should be very proud of him, and people should know he was your dad. I am very proud of what you did, and I am equally proud that you are the son of a hero. I really want people to know who your dad was and that he was awarded the

Medal of Honor. You have always avoided talking about your background when you should be bragging about it."

"Come on, Kay, it's great to know that my father saved the lives of three of his men, but we don't have to go around telling people about it."

"Anthony, it is high time you stop thinking of yourself as the illegitimate son of General Walker. He was your biological father. You are his son. You are Anthony Walker, son of General Bruce Walker, who was awarded the Congressional Medal of Honor."

Andrew spoke up. "Your mother was quite somebody too. Here, I have brought you a copy of the cover of an old issue of *Vogue* magazine. That's your mother on the cover. She was really beautiful. And here is a copy of a poster she did for the USO. No wonder your dad fell in love with her. After your dad died, she became a famous model. Too bad her career was cut short by that terrible disease. Anthony, both your parents were exceptional people. Kay is right, you should be very proud of them."

Andrew Spencer published the story under the title "Hero of Mohawk Flight 201 Has the Right DNA." After giving a detailed account of Anthony's rescue of Senator Rutherford's wife and son, Andrew went on to rave about the heroics of Anthony's father, General Walker. He used his own father's account of how the then-first lieutenant, risking his own life and despite being wounded, brought three of his men to safety. This account contained details, previously not commonly known, that had not been included in the recommendation for the Medal of Honor.

The article went on to talk about Anthony's mother, the beautiful Yuni. The story contained a picture of her on the cover of *Vogue* magazine and mentioned that she had been the famous model featured on a popular USO poster. Nowhere in the story was it mentioned that Anthony's father was not married to Yuni. The story ended with a long, drawn-out account of Anthony's wrestling career, which was cut short because of his heroic actions after the crash of Flight 201.

A week after the story appeared in print, Anthony received a strange telephone call.

"You would have been Dad's fourth child to make the Olympic team."

"Who is this, and what the heck are you talking about?"

"I am Bret Walker, your half brother. For a long time, I considered myself to be Dad's youngest son. But now I know you are my father's youngest son, and I want to meet you."

Anthony was totally confused. "I don't get it. Why do you think I'm your half brother?"

"From the magazine article by Andrew Spencer. He did not mention the rest of your family, but General Bruce Walker was also my father. He died when I was nineteen. We were living in Texas at the time, and my mother kept your existence and my father's romance with your mother a secret from me. After I read about you in the magazine, I was sure our father would have wanted us to meet. I still live in Texas, but if you agree, I could catch a plane to New Jersey next week and come visit you."

"Sure, that would be great," Anthony said. "Your call has totally caught me by surprise. My mom never mentioned my father's family, and as a kid, it never occurred to me that he might be married and have another family." When he hung up the phone, Anthony could not wait to tell Kay. The two of them were excited at the prospect of meeting Bret Walker. They immediately got on the Internet to find out as much as possible about Bret Walker and the rest of his family.

Bret Walker's engaging personality helped Anthony overcome his worries about meeting this total stranger who was his half-brother. What could have been a rather awkward introduction was handled very smoothly by Bret.

"Finally I get to meet my little brother, and he turns out to be half a foot taller than me. As you can see, I'm sort of the runt of the family." Anthony had to laugh. Bret was, indeed, quite a lot shorter than he. He had a stocky build, and his prematurely gray hair made him look a lot older.

"Yes, I'm the only one who took after my mother. Our older brother and sisters inherited our father's genes and are quite tall like you. But I'm jumping the gun. Let me first tell you a little about our family. When Dad graduated from West Point, he married my mom, Mary McPherson, the most-sought-after debutante in Texas.

"Despite her patrician upbringing, Mom adjusted quickly to life in the military and followed Dad from army base to army base. They had four children. Jack is the oldest, followed by Alice and Elisabeth. I am the youngest. Dad was promoted rapidly, and by the time I was fourteen, he was already a general, and we were living in Washington, DC. Dad was a striking figure. He was tall and very handsome, and he became very popular in social circles. Mom, who was always very reserved, could not keep up and chose to return to her home in Texas. After that the two of them grew apart, and when Dad received an overseas command, we saw very little of him.

"Mom died seven years ago. Jack and our sisters knew of your existence, but never mentioned anything to me. When I read the article about you and realized you are our half-brother, I confronted them as to why they had never attempted to contact you. They explained that they, like my mother, felt betrayed by our father's affair and refused to recognize your existence. In retrospect they can see how Dad must have felt alienated from his family, and they now have more empathy for his feelings toward your mother. If you can forgive their previous attitude toward you, they would like to meet you. As for me, when I saw the picture of your beautiful mother in the magazine, I could not blame Dad for falling in love with her. In all fairness, my mother had long before pushed him out of her life."

XXX

After the third operation on his feet, Anthony was very depressed. He had hoped to be able to walk by now, but he could not put any weight on his feet, and he was still wheelchair bound.

He was so depressed that one day he said to Kay, "If you don't want to be stuck with this cripple for the rest of your life, you don't have to marry me."

Kay was furious. "Don't ever say that again, not even in jest. You are everything to me, and I don't want to hear such stupid talk."

Anthony kept it up. "These damn feet, we can't even make love without them getting in the way!" Kay pushed his wheelchair into the bedroom. "What are you doing?"

"Just shut up and pull yourself onto the bed." When Anthony was lying on the bed, she undid his belt and pulled off his pants and shorts. Next she pulled off his shirt and quickly undressed herself. She got onto the bed and straddled him, her hands making him ready to receive her. Then she gently lowered herself on him.

"I want you and only you."

After they were both spent, she rolled off and lay next to him.

"Feel better now? I don't want to hear such talk again! The doctors say your feet are going to be fine. Before you know it, you'll be walking, but even if you could never walk again, I'll never leave you. We are in this together, and you are not getting rid of me."

Anthony rolled on his side and reached over to kiss her again. "You do love me, don't you, but I love you more." He laughed as Kay started their old game as to who loved whom the most.

It took two more operations before Anthony could walk, but from then on, it went fast, and by the beginning of the next year, Anthony could once again put on a normal pair of shoes.

Anthony and Kay did not waste the months it took for Anthony to recover. On their own they continued their studies. Kay would get assignments from their respective professors and then go to the library and pick out the books they needed. Although they could not get credit for the courses they completed, they had no trouble resuming their classroom studies after the Christmas vacation, and they both graduated in June with honors. Kay's mother could hardly wait. She had a huge June wedding in mind. The subject of their wedding had come up repeatedly in the past.

The discussion usually revolved around the problem of whether it should be a church wedding or not.

And if a church wedding, what religion? Neither Kay nor Anthony considered themselves part of an organized religion. If they were to go by their mothers' religion, they both should be Roman Catholics. Kay's mother had been brought up as a Roman Catholic, but had long ago abandoned the church. Like most people in the Philippines, Anthony's mother had been a Roman Catholic. But since she did not consider Anthony to be a Filipino, she did not bring him up as a Catholic. Kay's father was Jewish, but did not do much about it.

Kay's father summed it up for them: "Whatever you two choose to do, you won't get any resistance from us. Both of us consider our religion a moral code by which we try to live an ethical life. In that, there is absolutely no difference between your mother and me, despite the fact that we were brought up in different religions. From observing the two of you together, I know you share our values, and your commitment to each other will not depend on a church's blessing."

Eventually they decided on the following: They would invite the local mayor to perform the wedding, and two close friends of the family, one a rabbi and the other a Jesuit priest, would be asked to say a prayer and give a blessing.

Once this was decided, Kay's mother swung into action. Kay agreed to have the wedding take place at her parents' home. For the occasion the place was transformed into a virtual fairyland castle. The bills for the flowers, the caterers, the bands, and the serving staff were astronomical. The Goodmans did not care. Their only daughter was getting married to a man they adored. It was as much their day as it was Anthony and Kay's. Despite the fact that they were extremely honored by being asked to be best man and matron of honor, they approached Anthony with a special request. They knew Kay had also wanted to ask Rita and Jamal to be matron of honor and best man respectively, but she had preferred to give them the honor. They wanted Anthony to propose that there be two matrons of honor and two best men.

They were sure Anthony would love to ask Jamal to be best man, but they were not sure how he would feel about asking Rita to be the other matron of honor. When they spoke to Anthony, they were delighted to hear that he liked the idea. When Anthony told Kay how her parents felt, it was quickly decided that there would be two matrons of honor and two best men.

The rest of the bridal party consisted of Anthony's half-brothers and sisters, Bret, Jack, Alice and Elizabeth, Anthony's Princeton roommates, Tim, Doug and Adam, and Kay's longtime friend, Valerie Morgan. Three Princeton volleyball teammates rounded up the party. Kay was worried about the fact that Anthony had included his original three roommates.

"Remember how unhappy you were about the remarks they made about you and Rita? Are you sure you want them here, especially now that we have asked Rita to be one of the matrons of honor?"

"Don't worry, that is long buried. After they realized why I asked to move to another room, the three of them came to me to apologize. They told me they had been immature jerks. They were sorry I had left the room, but asked if we still could remain friends. I told them I was okay with that. As you know, they remained my closest pals on the wrestling team."

Inviting Adam Randall did create a problem. Right after graduation he had moved to California and contacted Sue-Ellen Worthingham. He was still obsessed with her sexy looks and her father's wealth. They had started dating, and Adam had asked if he could bring Sue-Ellen to the wedding as his date. Kay went through the roof.

"No way is he bringing that bitch to our wedding!"

Anthony was much more forgiving. "Kay, all of that is past history. I'm sure she has grown up by now. Remember, in her letter to me, she did say she was sorry about all the things she said."

"I told you then, and I will say it again, I don't care that she says she is sorry, I don't want to see that bitch ever again. You don't understand how deeply she hurt me. We had just met. And right from the beginning, I liked you a lot. We talked for a long time, and I felt very special about you. You were the first guy who seemed interested in me as a person. Not for my father's money or because I played on two college teams. You were interested in me, Kay Goodman! I always thought of myself as this tall, skinny, homely girl whom boys would rather make fun of than be caught dating. And then this Adonis and I had this wonderful conversation, and he seemed genuinely interested in me as a person. I felt like I got to look into your soul, and I saw gold. By the time we took that first walk in the park, I was deeply in love with you.

"But my roommate, Sue-Ellen, kept saying horrible things about you. What she said was meant to hurt you, but her words were like a dagger jammed into my heart. I can still feel the pain. Anthony, don't ask me to forgive her. I can't!"

Anthony agreed to tell Adam politely, but firmly, that Sue-Ellen was not welcome, but not before he said to Kay, "How could you possibly feel that way about yourself? When I first saw you, I thought you were good-looking, and when we started talking, you immediately made me feel comfortable. No girl had ever made me feel that way. I could easily have spent the rest of the afternoon talking to you."

Much different was the news they received from Rita. Several months after she returned to Nebraska, she had started dating her high school sweetheart, Russell Carter. She and Russell had dated through most of high school. When they graduated, he had joined the army, and she had left for New York. They promised to keep in contact, but Rita had stopped writing to Russell, and eventually he lost all contact with her.

After twenty years in the army, Russell retired and settled in his old hometown, Axel. During his years in the army, he had married twice and divorced twice. Back in Axel, he started his own insurance agency.

He was quite successful, not only writing insurance for the people in town, but also in the surrounding communities. Rita's cousin Betty made sure Rita met Russell soon after she returned to Axel. Russell claimed that the reason he had never stayed married and had gotten divorced twice was because he could never forget Rita. It did not take long before Rita moved in with Russell. Anthony and Kay were anxious to meet Russell, and they insisted that Rita bring him along to the wedding.

The weather on the day of the wedding was beautiful. The wedding was held outside in the gardens. Kay's mother had created a woodland grove, surrounded by masses of beautiful flowers, where the ceremony would take place. Kay came up with the idea that the entire wedding party would walk together from the house, through the guests seated on chairs on the lawn, to the wedding grove. Kay's mother and Rita looked beautiful, but both had been careful not to outshine Kay. Kay looked even better than she had at the engagement party.

When Jamal saw her all dressed up in her wedding gown, he could not help saying, "Man, you sure are one beautiful chick."

The reception following the wedding ceremony was held in large tents set up between the swimming pool and the tennis courts. That evening there was a seated dinner in the same tents, and the festivities lasted till deep into the night. The high point for many was the deeply moving blessing delivered during the wedding ceremony by the Jesuit priest. There was not a dry eye in the crowd by the time he ended with, "If Anthony's father and mother could have seen their son and his beautiful bride standing here before me, it would have strengthened and justified the deep love they felt for each other."

XXXI

*T**welve years later*
   "I am planning to transfer you to Chicago and
promote you to CEO of Transversal, our shopping
center subsidiary."

"Frank—sorry, I mean Dad—you must be kidding. Mind you, I don't mind moving to Chicago and
working for Transversal. But CEO? You must be
kidding!"

"I am dead serious, Anthony. You've earned your
spurs here. For the past ten years, you have helped
invigorate every one of our companies I placed you
in, and I need somebody to shake up Transversal."

"I really don't mind going to Transversal, but to
come in as the CEO is ridiculous."

"That's for me to decide, and it is not ridiculous.
They have been losing money for a couple of years.
I should have fired the CEO, Jeffrey Sloan, years ago.
To the detriment of the company, I have been much
too lenient with him. He's been with me for twenty
years, and he has supported me through thick and

thin, but he's done a lousy job at Transversal. The losses at Transversal are dragging the stock price of our company down. I am happy he has decided to retire."

"Like I said, I will be happy to go out there and see if we can't turn the place around, but to come in as CEO will cause resentment among the senior management."

"It probably will. Mark Waldman, the CFO, is expecting to be promoted to CEO once Jeffrey retires, but I know you can do a better job. Besides, if I don't send you to turn the place around, I will have to sell that company, and he would most likely be out of a job. We just can't afford to keep a losing outfit while our other divisions are doing so well. That would not be fair to our stockholders."

"And what do I do when I have to make changes, but Mark and the rest of the senior management don't agree with me?"

"You'll be their boss. Deal with it."

When Anthony came home that night and told Kay about his meeting with her dad, she was not surprised.

"Dad has great faith in your ability. If he thinks you can handle the CEO job, he would have no qualms about putting you in that job. Like it or not, he will put you ahead of others if he thinks he can justify his decision. Lately, he has relied on you more and more to put out some fires for him. And so far you have not failed to produce."

"Yeah, yeah, like everybody won't know that the only reason I got the job was that I am Frank's son-in-law."

"That, my dear husband, is pure hogwash. You graduated cum laude from Princeton, and you have an MBA from Wharton. Dad never babied you. He assigned you to some of the nastiest problems within the conglomerate, and you handled them. You can do it! Chicago, here we come."

"I'll never have the excuse that I had a wife who held me back. If I weren't married to you already, I'd ask you to be my wife right now!"

"You'd have a tough time explaining the twins."

"Yes, the twins. How will they adjust to another new school?"

"Anthony, they are healthy eight-year-old girls. They'll adjust."

XXXII

"**M**r. Walker, sir, your wife is on the phone."
"What line, please?"

"She is holding on your private line. Please push button four."

"Kay, what's the matter? The kids okay?"

"Kids are fine. It's about Jamal."

"What about him? Was he in an accident?"

"No, but his mother just called. He's been arrested."

"What the hell for?"

"Don't know, but she wants you to help."

"Where is he now?"

"No idea, she did not give me any details. She was crying hysterically and repeatedly asked for you to help him."

"I'll see what I can find out." Anthony hung up the phone and buzzed for Nancy, his secretary, to come into his office.

"Nancy, please call the Seattle Buccaneers. That's a professional basketball team. Try to get a responsible person on the phone, the manager, or the coach, or somebody I can speak to about the arrest of one of their players. Oh yes, assure them that I am not a reporter."

It seemed to take forever, but finally Nancy called. "I have Sid McClellan, their general manager, on the phone. Here he comes."

"Hello, Mr. McClellan. I am Anthony Walker, and I'm calling from Chicago to find out what is going on with Jamal Griffin."

"You family of his?"

"No, he's one of my best friends."

"Well, if you're not family, don't worry about it. We'll take care of the matter."

"Just tell me where he is."

"The police will release a full report in a couple of hours that should give you all the details. In the meantime our lawyers will take care of everything."

"I'm certainly glad your lawyers are involved, but can you please tell me where he is and which police department will issue the report?"

"He is being held in the city jail. It's near the Spiral. The metro police will give a press conference at five o'clock."

"Thank you for the information."

When he hung up, Anthony called his father-in-law in the New York office. "Dad, my friend Jamal has been arrested."

"What for?"

"Don't know. All I know so far is that he is being held in the city jail in Seattle and that the police will hold a press conference at five o'clock, their time. I want to go out there and see what exactly is going on, but I have a very important meeting tomorrow."

"What's the meeting about?"

"We are negotiating to buy a shopping mall on the west side of town."

"Your staff is fully briefed on the project?"

"Yes, I have had a team working on this project for over four months."

"Good. Who is your point man, and is he good?"

"It's Billy Freedman. He's one of my best."

"Go to Seattle to help your friend. I'll fly to Chicago to take your place. Be sure to leave me all the powers of attorney I need in case we clinch the deal."

XXXIII

"Anthony, how the hell did you get in here?"

"It's not how I got in here. It's how the fuck did you wind up in this jail?"

"They got it all wrong. They plan to charge me with disorderly conduct and possession of an illegal weapon."

"Great, what exactly happened?"

"Man, what a mess. I took my younger sister and her friend out for a night on the town. We were going to celebrate her birthday. She turned twenty-one and can now legally drink, so we headed for the Golden Slipper. You probably never heard of it, but it's a pretty ritzy club in the downtown area. I have to admit both girls were dressed pretty provocatively. Anyway, I had reserved a good table. When we were on our way to our seats, a drunk started to call after us. To be exact, he said, 'Look at those pieces of ass. Boy, would I like some of that.' I ignored him, but he kept on. 'Hey, fellow, why don't you share? You don't need two. And I would love to have a piece of that black tail.' I turned around and decked him. I guess I hit him a little too hard, because he went flying across two tables, spilling drinks all over the people sitting there.

"The management called the cops. And because not everyone heard what the bastard said, they thought I started the ruckus. The cops took me outside and frisked me. They found the gun I always carry for protection and took me straight to the police station."

"Why the hell do you carry a gun?"

"Are you kidding, why? For protection! Man, ever since I signed that eight-year, hundred-million-dollar contract, I have been robbed at least four times. Those idiots think I carry the cash on me! Anyway, I have all the licenses they require, but that still does not allow anyone to carry a gun into a bar. I forgot about that, and the club is considered a bar."

"What happened to the girls?"

"They went home by taxi; I want to keep them out of this."

"I appreciate that, but we might need them to prove what that drunk said that made you deck him."

"Now that you know how I wound up in here, how did you get here so fast?"

"Your mom called to tell us you were arrested. I had to see for myself what was going on. I had corporate out of New York set me up with some lawyers here in town. As we speak, they are conferring with the law firm the Buccaneers engaged for you."

"And where does that leave me?"

"They'll make sure you have a bail hearing in the morning, and we'll get you the hell out of here."

"Can I leave tonight?"

"We tried, but the best we could do was a hearing early in the morning. The judge will probably set a pretty steep amount for bail, but it isn't likely he will consider you a flight risk. Anyway, not for what you have been charged with."

The next morning the lawyers came to court fully prepared to have the disorderly conduct charge dropped. They had dug up four witnesses who were willing to testify that the drunk had provoked the scuffle. Jamal was released on bail, but he still had to face the weapons charge. Rather than wait for a trial date, the lawyers immediately started negotiating with the DA's office to also drop that charge. They argued that Jamal had never owned any ammunition for the gun he carried, and that he would have been alerted to the fact that it was forbidden to carry the gun into the club if a sign indicating that had been properly posted at the entrance.

The owner of the nightclub, an acquaintance of Jamal's, took it upon himself to contact the DA's office and explain that after the last restoration, they had neglected to replace the sign. The sign was still in storage, and he felt the charges against Jamal should be dismissed. He made a point of the fact that Jamal never even attempted to draw the gun, not even to scare the man who had made the highly provocative remarks. He wondered why the man had not been charged with making those clearly racist remarks.

Anthony had been back in Chicago for more than a week when Jamal called to tell him that all charges had been dropped.

"I hope you have learned something from this and gotten rid of that damn gun."

"You sound like my mother and grandmother. Yes, I have gotten rid of it."

"Jamal, don't you think it's about time to settle down? You're in your thirties and still dating like a high school kid."

"Now you do sound like my mother and grandmother. But dammit, it's not as easy as you think. Sure, I got lots of girls running after me. And yes, they are all beautiful, sexy, and all that. Some of them even have some brains in their head, but they don't really give a damn about me. They adore the big basketball star, and it doesn't hurt that he is very rich, but they don't bother to know the real me. You know me. I don't like all that phoniness around me. Girls dying to crawl into my bed, just to become part of that star-filled scene."

Anthony smiled. Regardless of his success, Jamal had not changed. He was still his well-grounded roommate.

"Don't laugh when I say it, but do I have a girl for you."

"What on earth are you taking about?"

"Remember that girl at our wedding? Kay's friend, the one you danced with all night?"

"Sure I do."

"I should think so. You spent so much time with her that Kay's young niece was miffed that she never got to dance with you."

"I'm sorry; you should have said something to me."

"Don't worry about it. I was happy enough with the fact that you went out of your way to dance with Aunt Rita and tell her all was okay now."

"What about this girl?"

"Oh yeah, Valerie. The one who was tall enough not to be dwarfed by you, the one with the figure that made you drool. Well, my dear friend, she is single again, and I think she would be perfect for you."

"What do you mean by single again?"

"She recently got out of a real abusive relationship. About three years after our wedding, she married Thomas Elgin, the Scandinavian movie star. You may remember him. He was a big deal a few years back. Unfortunately for him, his career fizzled, while she shot up the corporate ranks at Shell Oil. The more successful she became, the more he resented her for it. He started blaming her career for his failure. He became more and more abusive, and she finally left him. They were divorced about a year ago."

"And you think she would be interested in me?"

"The way the two of you got along at my wedding, I would say yes."

"She is gorgeous, but what makes you say she is perfect for me?"

"She is a real person. Like you once said to me, you don't let that type of girl get away. She is real, or she would not have been Kay's best friend all this time. Besides, your family won't object. She is African American."

"And you want me to just pick up the phone and say, 'Hi, I'm Jamal. You may not remember me, but Anthony says you are the perfect girl for me.'"

"Yeah, something like that. You could add, 'I think you're beautiful, and I have not stopped thinking about you since the time we met at Kay's wedding.'"

"You've got to be kidding!"

"Of course I am! But I have a plan. Frank, my father-in-law, has a box at Madison Square Garden for all the Knicks games. If you let me know when you will be in NY to play the Knicks, I'll arrange for Kay, Valerie, and me to be at the game. After the game we'll all go out to dinner together. And the rest is up to you."

XXXIV

"Of course you can have the box for the fifteenth. I want you and Kay to stay over and spend the night with us in Deal. I need you in the office the next day."

"That would be great, Dad. Why do you need me?"

"Not over the phone. And I don't want to discuss it at the house. We'll just treat it as a routine issue until we are alone at my office."

On the morning after the game Frank's chauffeur picked them up before seven, and they beat the rush into the City. They parked in the building and took the elevator up to Frank's office on the thirty-third floor. Anthony was somewhat apprehensive as to what Frank wanted to talk to him about. Frank wasted no time getting started.

"You know, of course, of the proxy battle that an activist shareholders fund is trying to start."

"I am aware of that, but you told me they had absolutely no chance of gaining control because you have eighteen percent of the stock and forty percent of the voting shares."

"All that is true, but something has come up that might work in their favor. They could force me out."

"What do you mean by they could force you out?"

"Yolanda Evans has filed a sexual harassment suit against me. She is the young lady who substituted for Mrs. Gilmore, my longtime private secretary, while she was recovering from breast cancer."

"Sexual harassment suit? You must be kidding!"

"I wish I were! She claims that from the moment she started working for me, I made unwanted sexual advances. Worse than that, she claims I forced myself on her and threatened to fire her if she did not cooperate. In the suit she claims to have had forced sex with me on several occasions, here in the office and on the company airplane."

"That's ludicrous. Nobody will believe her."

"That's what I thought, but now she has come up with two people who will corroborate her claim."

"Oh come on, Frank. What's she claiming? Group sex here in the office?"

"Anthony, this is very serious. I wish it were just some bad joke or a disturbed young lady making up ridiculous stories. Two days ago Richard Herman came to see me. You know him; he's a partner at Kevel, Patrick, and Douglas, the law firm the company uses. He told me Yolanda claims that Betty Sawyer, the receptionist here on the executive floor, and Arthur Spear, the steward on our company plane, are willing to testify on her behalf."

"Testify to what? That they stood by and watched? Frank, this is just plain ridiculous. Anybody who has seen Mom knows there is no way you would get involved with a girl like Yolanda, let alone force her to have sex. Let her sue. She'll be laughed out of court!"

"That was my first reaction, but Richard Herman does not think so. He thinks a jury might be sympathetic toward her. You know, young single woman up against powerful corporate CEO. He says her lawyer will claim that rich executives presume they are entitled, and they think they are above the law. Richard advised me to try to settle this case as quickly as possible and to take my chances in a proxy battle. He says we can argue that we settled for convenience, that it was a harassment suit without factual basis."

"Don't you dare give in! The whole thing is just a slimy way to extort money!"

"I agree with you, but I think we should follow Richard's advice: settle quickly and get the whole affair behind us as soon as possible. That way, it will be old news by the time they get the proxy battle going."

"No way. You're not going to let them smirch your reputation. You're the most honorable man I know, and I won't allow it."

"Hold on, Anthony. I really appreciate your sticking up for me, but this is not a personal decision. It's a business decision. It won't do the company any good to have the CEO go through a long drawn-out court fight on a sexual harassment charge. Besides, as Richard has pointed out, we might lose. No, Richard is right. We have to settle this thing as quickly as possible. The truth is not important here."

"You're wrong. The truth is everything. I know you well enough to know that none of what she claims is even remotely possible. You did not harass or touch her. That has to be our standpoint, because it is the truth. Plus, this is not a business decision. This is personal."

"Anthony, I really appreciate your concern for my reputation. But these things happen in business, and it is one of the risks we have to accept. High-profile executives are often a target for people out for a quick buck. It comes with the territory, and a lot of people will look on it that way when we settle this claim. There is always a chance that I could lose a proxy fight, but if I settle this harassment suit, I have a much better chance of winning the proxy battle than if I get involved in a court case and fight this case in public."

"Frank, I know this is your decision, but I'll fight you on it. This does not only involve the company. It also involves Mom, your granddaughters, my children, Kay, and even me. You owe it to us to fight this phony accusation. And most of all, you owe it to yourself. I know you wanted to keep this quiet as long as possible, but I would like to discuss this with Mom and Kay tonight at dinner."

"I think I have pretty well made up my mind to follow Richard's advice, but you're right. I should let them know about this before anything leaks out. I wanted to tell Sue before, but I did not know how. She considers the company as one big family much more than I do. She won't understand how one of our employees could make such an allegation against me. I was counting on your support to help explain that it is not that unusual for this to happen in large companies when a greedy person sees deep pockets."

"I agree with you that suits like this are not that uncommon, but I disagree with the idea that it is best to settle."

"Okay, we'll discuss it further at dinner."

The subject was not touched on during the drive home, as the driver could hear every word they said. It was not till after dinner that Frank started discussing the pending proxy fight, and from there, he carefully led into the sexual harassment suit.

"That bitch, how dare she?" Sue's voice was shaking. "We should sue her back, get her locked up for lying, for slander."

"Hold on, Sue." Frank tried to calm her down. "Richard Herman, one of our lawyers, says this type of claim is an attempt to extort some cash, and is not that uncommon in today's business environment. He recommends we settle and get the whole affair out of the way before the proxy vote takes place."

"No way. We are going to take that fucking bitch down. Settle! Are you crazy? We are not going to reward her for those dirty lies."

Anthony had never seen Sue like this, nor had he ever heard her use such strong language; her face had turned red, and her eyes were blazing.

"Mom, I agree with you, but we can't just call her a liar. We have to prove she lied. It might be difficult, but I am sure we can do it."

Kay did not agree. "How do we go about proving she made the whole thing up? It's going to be hard, especially since she claims to have those two witnesses."

"They'll never testify on her behalf, I know that," Sue said. "Arthur may be a little wimpy, but he is always very friendly and helpful when I fly on the plane. And Betty Sawyer, definitely not. I have known her for a long time, and we always discuss her mom when I come in the office. As a matter of fact, about six months ago, I helped get her mother into a better long-term care facility."

Kay was not convinced. "That does not guarantee anything. You never know what motivates someone to do the unexpected. Maybe it's best to settle. Dad, what would that involve?"

"The company would deny the charges in the strongest terms and at the same time, start bargaining with Yolanda's lawyer as to the amount they would accept to drop the case."

Kay turned to Anthony. "Why don't you think that would be the best solution?"

Before Anthony could answer, Sue spoke. "Never! We are not going to settle this. We'll expose her for the liar she is. Imagine giving her money when all she is, is a dirty blackmailer."

Frank realized he was not going to get Sue to agree with him, and he turned to Anthony.

"Of course, this would have to be discussed at a board of directors meeting at the company, but since Sue and you seem dead set against settling, how would you proceed? You're sure we can prove she is lying? How would you do that?"

"I haven't the slightest idea, but I'll be damned if I'll give in without trying," Anthony said. "Can I have a week before you definitively decide what to do?"

Frank and Sue answered at the same time. "Yes."

They decided Kay would return the next day to Chicago, while Anthony stayed to look deeper into the case.

XXXV

Anthony realized he needed a strong ally inside the company to help him disprove the charges against his father-in-law. The logical choice was Mrs. Gilmore. She had fully recovered from breast cancer and was back at her old job. As soon as he arrived at the office, he went to see her.

"Margaret, I need your help. Yolanda Evans, the young lady who took your place during your illness, has filed a sexual harassment suit against Frank."

"That's not funny, Anthony. I have no time for cruel jokes."

"You know me well enough to know I would never joke about something like this. It's true."

"Oh my God, she must be crazy. Of all people, against Frank. Impossible!"

"That's the way I feel, and I need your help to prove she is lying. We need to prove that this is no more than a filthy way to extort money from the company."

"A sexual harassment suit against Frank. Oh my, this would never have happened if I had not gotten sick."

"That's ridiculous. You certainly could not help getting sick, and the people in HR could not know that the woman they hired to replace you was such a bad person."

"What does Frank say about this?"

"He has been advised by our company lawyers to settle and get this affair out of the way as soon as possible, but I don't agree."

"Settle? But that is impossible. I have known your father-in-law longer than anyone else in this company, and those allegations cannot be true. Frank would never do such a thing. Never!"

"That's why I want to prove she is lying. I have contacted a private investigator, and he'll be here any moment. I told him to ask for direction to your office when he arrives. Have him sent up here immediately."

A few minutes later, Jarrod McNeese arrived. "I am looking for a Mr. Anthony Walker."

"That's me; come on in." Jarrod McNeese did not look at all like Anthony expected. He was casually dressed in well-worn jeans and a blue dress shirt open at the collar. His brush cut was much too young for a man of his age, but he came with great references. Anthony wasted no time on formalities.

"The claims made in the sexual harassment suit we talked about on the phone are fabricated. We need you get us as much background information as you can on that Yolanda Evans woman who instigated the suit. We need to know if the purpose of the suit is purely financial, or if she has some other motives we are not aware of. We also need more information on Arthur Spear and Betty Sawyer. Supposedly, they are two witnesses who will corroborate Yolanda's allegations."

"Interesting. Did they stand by and watch it, or did they participate?"

"I already made a joke about that to my father-in-law. We don't have any idea what they will say. They have not yet been deposed by our lawyers, who happen to favor settling the case. Arthur Spear is the steward on the company airplane, and Betty Sawyer works in reception.

"Mrs. Gilmore will give you any information the company has on them. She will be your only contact here at the company. Nobody else has been told about this. One other thing: I also would like you to look into Green Acre Investment, the activist shareholders fund that wants to replace the management of this company by calling for a proxy vote. I want to know who really holds the purse strings there."

"Looks like I don't have to travel outside the city, so it won't take me too long to get all the information you are looking for. Don't be surprised if I find more than you expect. I'm really good. Anyway, you would not have hired me if you didn't know that."

Anthony had to laugh at Jarrod's total lack of modesty. "I guess that accounts for your fees being about twice what other investigators charge. Don't worry, I am not haggling; I am relying on you not to miss a thing. A lot is at stake. I have to return to Chicago, but as I said before, you can contact Mrs. Gilmore for anything you need. And you have my home and cell phone. Here is a check to cover your retainer. Also, I have written down my home address so you can send me your declaration."

After Jarrod left, Mrs. Gilmore asked if Frank was aware that Anthony had hired a private eye to investigate Yolanda and the two witnesses.

"He knows I don't agree with the lawyers," Anthony said. "I told him we should never settle, and he knows I am trying to prove that Yolanda is lying. But no, he does not know I hired Jarrod."

"Anthony, I so hope this Jarrod character can come up with something. He does not look very professional. Do you really trust him?"

When he saw tears welling up in Margaret's eyes, Anthony tried to reassure her, "Don't worry, Margaret. I made a thorough check; he's the best in his field."

By now Margaret was crying. "They can't do this to Frank. It's so unfair."

"Don't cry, Margaret. It's going to be all right."

"You don't understand. Your father-in-law has been my mentor since I was a young girl. He is much more than that. He lent us the down payment when we bought our first house. When Jimmy, my husband, was involved in that terrible car accident and became disabled, he stood by us. He helped with the medical bills, and when Jimmy could no longer do the work and lost his job, he raised my salary so we still would be comfortable. Anthony, that man is everything to me. Promise me you'll show the world he did not touch that...that whore. Anthony, you must do this for Frank and for Sue and...for all of us who love him."

Listening to Margaret, Anthony felt the full weight of the obligation he had taken on by persuading Frank to let him try to disprove Yolanda's allegations.

Anthony's next stop that day was at the law offices of Kevel, Patrick, and Douglas. He had been sitting in the reception room for about ten minutes when a good-looking young man dressed in a stylish pinstriped suit approached him and stuck out his hand in greeting.

"Hi, I am Isaiah Gibson. You must be Anthony Goodman. Richard Herman has been called away, and he asked me to meet with you."

"Actually, my name is Anthony Walker. I am Frank Goodman's son-in-law, and I made an appointment with Richard Herman, the senior partner responsible for the Goodman Industries account. By the way, I am also CEO of Transversal, the second-largest subsidiary of Goodman Industries."

"Great, I am starting with three strikes against me. I did not know your name. I did not know your position in the company. And on top of that, you came to see my boss, not me. I'm really sorry, but Richard only told me that Frank Goodman's son was coming to discuss his decision to delay the settlement talks for the sexual harassment case we are working on."

"Yeah, and Richard does not agree, so he does not want to talk to me. He sends you."

"Look, I am only a lowly associate here, so don't expect me to question Richard's motives. He told me he was called away on an urgent matter and asked me to meet with you in his stead."

"Actually, that is not a bad idea; I don't really feel like arguing with Richard, and as the senior partner here, he probably feels he should only deal with Frank. I want you to start preparing to fight this suit. It is not in the best interest of Frank or the company to settle this case. Since there is no factual basis for the lady's claim, we should not even think of settling. I'll get Frank to agree that you take the lead on this case."

"That's very flattering, but Richard will never agree to that. Goodman Industries is one of our major clients, and they won't let an associate take the lead on this case."

"Richard should have thought of that before he sent you to meet with me. I'll make sure you are appointed to work with me. I have hired a private investigator to give us a complete background on all the witnesses, and I'll give you that information before you depose them. That will include Yolanda Evans, the woman who has filed the suit. I don't want these allegations to linger too long, and I want you to arrange for a trial as soon as possible."

Anthony took the late-afternoon plane back to Chicago. When he got there, he called Jim Cullen, his stockbroker. Jim had already left his office, so he called him at home.

"Jim, I have something very special I want you do for me."

"As long as it does not involve some inside information that might affect your holding of Goodman Industries stock, I'm all ears."

"Now that you mention it, it could. Some little rat is suing Frank, my father-in-law, for sexual harassment. That, of course, could affect Goodman Industries stock, so you and I cannot be involved in any stock transaction involving the company until this news becomes public."

"Jesus, that is pretty serious. How is the company going to handle it?"

"The company lawyers want to settle, but we are going to fight it."

"Okay, agreed, no trades. What can I do for you?"

"Awhile back, Salvos Industries made a hostile bid to take over Goodman Industries. They failed because Frank owns forty percent of the voting stock. But Henry Buchanan, their chairman, swore he would find a way to get his hands on Goodman Industries. A few months ago, Green Acre Investment, an activist shareholders fund, initiated a proxy battle to gain control of the Goodman Industries board. They are well aware that it is impossible to win as long as Frank holds so many of the voting shares. Then out of the blue comes this sexual harassment suit. I smell a rat. They are out to discredit Frank and make him resign. I am just guessing, and I can't prove a thing. But I would like you to search for a possible connection between Henry Buchanan and Green Acre Investment."

"That won't be easy. Henry Buchanan might be a bastard, but he is very clever. I'll try my best to see what I can come up with."

XXXVI

"Anthony, it's all over the TV. I'm afraid the kids will see it."

"Yeah, I know. Yolanda's lawyer is determined to try the case in the press. They are giving interviews to every reporter willing to give them favorable coverage. But I was happy to see that Isaiah is not letting them get away with it. He has managed to get Mrs. Gilmore on the late news in New York City. She gave a tearful testimonial in which she described your father as a saint, incapable of harassing anyone."

"All well and good, but what do I tell the girls?"

"Tell them the truth, that the whole thing has been dreamed up to get money from the company."

"That's not what they will hear at school. And Mom and Dad are also getting rattled by all the publicity. Dad is starting to worry that he made a mistake in not going ahead and settling the case."

"I think that is more Richard Herman talking than Dad losing faith in our ability to discredit Yolanda.

Thanks to Jarrod, we now know Betty Sawyer has financial troubles, and Arthur Spear has been trying to get the company to pay for his pilot training."

"That does not necessarily prove they are lying."

"True. Jarrod is digging deeper to see if this has any bearing on their testimony and if we can discredit them as witnesses."

"Anthony, I'm really getting worried that this is going the wrong way. I know Dad did not do anything to that woman, but how do we prove that? So far, we have nothing concrete to go on."

"If I were not so absolutely sure your father did not touch Yolanda, I too would be worried. But I know somehow the truth will come out, and we'll prove she is lying."

The tension mounted as the trial date approached, and even Anthony had to admit that Yolanda's side was winning in public opinion. To make matters worse, Goodman Industries' stock dropped more than 10 percent and was still sliding when the trial opened. On the first day, Yolanda proved to be a great witness. With great emotion, she described how Frank had started by touching her breasts, and when she pushed his hand away, he just smiled and continued to unbutton her shirt. She claimed he ignored her protests and told her that if she wanted to keep her job, she had better be nice to him. She got even more emotional when she described the day he put his hand on her thigh, pushed up her skirt, and put his hand in her panties. She claimed she begged him to stop as he pulled off her panties and got on top of her. Fear of losing her job made her lie still and let him have his way with her.

Isaiah did his best on cross-examination. "Miss Evans, how long did you work at Goodman Industries?"

"Thirteen months."

"And you claim you endured sexual harassment at the hands of Frank Goodman during much of this time? You have also stated that you willingly endured this alleged harassment out of fear of losing your job."

Yolanda's lawyer jumped to his feet. "She did not willingly submit to his harassment."

The judge partly agreed, but since Yolanda did not claim physical violence, he let Isaiah continue. "You came to Goodman Industries through Vadior, a temp agency, is that right?"

"Yes sir."

"And how long did you work for Vadior?"

Again Yolanda's lawyer objected. "Her employment at Vadior is not relevant in this case."

Isaiah said he would show that it was, and the judge allowed it. "Now, Miss Evans, how long have you worked for Vadior?"

"I don't know exactly, but I have been with them at least for five years."

"And all that time, you were employed at various companies that required temporary help?"

"Yes."

"And during those five-plus years, what was the longest period in which Vadior could not find a job for you?"

"Objection," her attorney protested. "Her employment through Vadior has no relevance to what happened to my client at Goodman Industries."

"Overruled. Continue, Mr. Gibson."

"I can't say," Yolanda said. "I did not keep track."

"Well, let me help you. Here are your employment records from Vadior. They show that except for several short vacations, you never went more than two weeks without being sent out on a new assignment. So why were you so afraid of losing the job at Goodman Industries?"

"I've never been let go, and I was afraid of losing my good employment record."

"Miss Evans, how long ago did your temporary employment at Goodman Industries end?"

"About four months ago."

"And during that time, you have found steady employment via Vadior?"

"Yes sir, I'm very good at my job."

"I'm sure you are, but it was not until a few weeks ago that you decided to file this harassment suit. For almost four months, you had no fear of losing your job, yet you did not file your suit until very recently. Miss Evans, I put it to you that there never was any harassment. No further questions!"

On redirect, Yolanda's lawyer tried to correct the damage. Yolanda kept insisting her testimony was true. She claimed she did not file a suit for harassment because she was too embarrassed to tell anyone. It was not until she confided in a close friend that the friend persuaded her to file suit.

Arthur Spear testified that on a flight to California, he heard Yolanda repeatedly say, "Please don't do that." Isaiah asked him where he was when he supposedly heard this. "I was in the galley preparing drinks."

"And where was Yolanda when you heard this?"

"She was in Frank's office."

"Where is that office?"

"It's in the back of the plane."

"I see, and the galley is in the front, right behind the pilots, isn't that right?"

"Yes, that is correct."

"That plane must have extremely silent engines for you to hear what was going on all the way in the back of the plane. No further questions!"

The next witness was Betty Sawyer, and it appeared that Isaiah did manage to discredit her. She testified that she saw Yolanda come out of Frank's office; her clothes were disheveled, and her makeup was smeared. According to Betty, Yolanda ran down the hall to the nearest bathroom. Isaiah pointed out that Frank's private office had a beautiful bathroom. If Yolanda did not want to report the alleged sexual assault, for fear of losing her job, why not use the private bathroom, rather than run in the hall in the disheveled state described by Betty?

At the end of the first day of the trial, Isaiah was pretty optimistic, but Richard Herman was not so sure. He felt what Isaiah had presented so far was not strong enough to disprove Yolanda's claim, and that the jury would side with Yolanda. Isaiah told him Jarrod McNeese had called him to tell him he had important new information. They had an appointment to meet later that evening.

XXXVII

O n the second day of the trial, Isaiah recalled
Arthur Spear.

"Mr. Spear, you always wanted to be a pilot, but
could not afford pilot school, is that right?" Yolanda's
lawyer objected, but Isaiah assured the judge he
would show this was relevant. When Arthur agreed
this was true, Isaiah continued, "Is it not true, Mr.
Spear, that last month you enrolled in pilot's school
and paid for three months in advance?"

"Yes, I have been saving for that."

"Then why is it that six months ago you requested
a loan from Goodman Industries in order to pay for
pilot school? I put it to you that in six months, you
could not possibly have saved enough to pay for
three months of pilot school. No further questions."

Yolanda's lawyer could do little to help explain
Arthur's recent acquisition of the money. Next,
Isaiah recalled Betty Sawyer.

"Miss Sawyer, your mother is in a long-term care facility, is that correct?" Yolanda's lawyer did not even bother to object.

"Yes, she is," Betty said.

"And as recently as three months ago, you were seriously behind in your payments to this long-term care facility, and you were also behind on the rent for your apartment."

"Yes, but I have paid it all. I have no debts."

"Precisely, you have paid everything in the last month and seem to live comfortably, despite the fact that your salary has not increased during that time."

"I forgot to pay my bills, but I have the money to pay all of them."

"Yes, apparently you do. No further questions." Again, Yolanda's lawyer could not get Betty to give an explanation as to how she obtained the money to pay her debts.

Now it was Yolanda's turn to retake the stand. "Miss Evans, do you know a gentleman called Milford Emmens?"

"Yes, he is my fiancé."

"And did you and Mr. Emmens purchase a condominium very recently?"

"Yes, we did."

"And how much was the purchase price and how much down payment did the two of you make?"

"I don't remember. I am not good at figures. My fiancé takes care of those things. He handled the whole thing."

"That's really hard to believe, but to help you remember, we will call Mr. Emmens to the stand." Isaiah turned to the judge. "With the court's permission, we would like to call Mr. Milford Emmens as a hostile witness."

Yolanda's lawyer objected, since Isaiah had not given notice he would call upon Emmens. The judge agreed to a recess of several days so Milford Emmens could be served with a summons to appear in court, which would give the plaintiff's lawyer a change to prepare.

Milford Emmens was quite hostile when Isaiah started to question him. "Mr. Emmens, could you please tell this court the name of your employer."

"I work for an investment fund."

"I'm sure this investment fund has a name."

Grudgingly Emmens said, "Green Acre Investments."

"And what is your position there?"

"I am the CEO and chief investment officer."

"And in your position as CEO of Green Acre Investments, have you ever heard of Mr. Henry Buchanan?"

"Yes."

"I can barely hear you; could you speak a little louder?"

"Yes, I know him."

"Could you describe your relation with Mr. Buchanan?"

"He has shares in Green Acre Investment."

"Do you have any other connection to Mr. Buchanan?"

"No, he is a major shareholder in our fund."

"Mr. Emmens, I remind you that you are under oath. Now, what other relationship exists between you and Mr. Buchanan?" Emmens looked at the plaintiff's lawyer as if asking for help. "Mr. Emmens, once more, what other connection exists between you and Mr. Henry Buchanan?"

"As I told you, he is a major shareholder in Green Acre."

"Okay, let me put it this way. Is it not true that Henry Buchanan gave you the money to buy the condo you and your fiancée, Yolanda Evans, recently purchased?"

"He lent us the money, yes. But it was a business transaction between us."

"Mr. Emmens, I again remind you that you are still under oath. Is it not true that Mr. Buchanan is the chairman of Salvos Industry, and in that capacity gave you the money in exchange for your promise to have the Green Acre Investment Fund engage in a proxy battle with Goodman Industries?"

Yolanda's lawyer desperately tried to stop this line of questioning, but the judge told him to sit down, and Isaiah continued.

"Mr. Emmens, there was more to your agreement with Mr. Buchanan, was there not?"

"No, there was not. It was strictly a businesslike loan and had nothing to do with any proxy battle my fund has engaged in."

"Mr. Emmens, we know there was more to the agreement. It was not a loan. It was in exchange for starting the proxy battle and for having your fiancée, Yolanda Evans, file a sexual harassment suit against Frank Goodman. Isn't it true that Mr. Buchanan is out to destroy the credibility of Frank Goodman?"

Before Milford Emmens could answer, all hell broke loose in the courtroom. Reporters jumped up and ran for the telephones. The judge could hardly be heard as he loudly called for order. When the crowd calmed down, Isaiah asked the judge for a directed verdict. The judge agreed to rule on the motion and recessed the court until he could reach a decision. He ordered the lawyers for both sides to join him in his chambers.

When court resumed, the judge directed a verdict for the defendant and announced that the DA's office would be looking into the relationship between Henry Buchanan and Milford Emmens and his fiancée, Yolanda Evans.

After Frank and his family had stopped hugging and kissing one another in celebration of the verdict, Richard Herman came over to Anthony.

"Big gamble, but you were right. This outcome is so much better than if we had settled. You have good instincts."

"I know my father-in-law. We had no choice but to prove he could not do such a thing."

The next day on the plane back to Chicago, Kay turned to her husband. "Anthony, were you ever in doubt?"

"Are you kidding? Of course I was. I didn't know we would win until I heard what Jarrod McNeese found out."

Kay opened her purse and took out a letter addressed to Anthony. "Dad asked me to give you this." Anthony took the letter, opened the blank envelope, and pulled out his father-in-law's beautifully embossed stationery. He read the short handwritten note, and his eyes started tearing up.

"What's wrong?" Kay asked.

Anthony read the note to her.

"I will retire at the end of the month and am nominating you to be my successor as CEO of Goodman Industries.

Love,

Dad"

XXXVIII

The move back to New York City was a lot more complicated than Anthony and Kay had anticipated. The problems started when the twins objected to moving in the middle of a school year. Both parents considered their objection quite reasonable. They all decided that Kay and the girls would stay remain in Chicago until the end of the school year. Anthony would go ahead and move into a hotel near his office until the rest of the family could join him.

On the night before Anthony left, one of the twins knocked on their bedroom door. Kay opened the door. "What's the matter Jessie? Can't you sleep?"

"Can I come in? I have to talk to you two."

"Sure, come on in. What's up?"

"Mom, Dad it's about Jackie".

Anthony jumped out of bed. "Jessie what happened, what is wrong with Jackie?" Anthony asked as he was heading out the door on the way to Jackie's bedroom.

Jessie stopped him. "No Dad, just listen to me!!" Jessie was crying when she blurted out, "She's my best friend. I don't want to rat on her but I have to tell you something before Daddy leaves for New York."

Kay gave Anthony a questioning look and quickly put her arm around Jessie. "Oh Honey don't cry. Come sit on the bed and tell us what is going on. You know it's always okay to tell us everything. If it's important it isn't ratting on your sister to tell us what is going on." Kay guided Jessie to the bed.

Jessie stopped crying, but still looked very uncomfortable when she blurted out. "Jackie has been hanging out with the wrong crowd."

"And you're not part of that crowd?" Anthony asked.

"I am not!" Jessie shot back.

"You feel left out and are a little jealous?" Kay carefully suggested.

"I'm not jealous!" Jessie screamed back at her. "Listen to me!" The sobbing had stopped and Jessie was angry. "I am not part of that crowd. I don't want to be friends with them. They do drugs. If you two knew what the hell was going on with your daughters, you would know that Jackie does drugs. Yes, damn it, my sister does drugs. I can't stop her, and you two are too busy to notice."

It was hard to tell who was more shocked. Kay and Anthony both rushed to embrace their daughter.

Kay had both arms around her as she pulled Jessie to her chest. "I'm sorry, so sorry. Baby, we let you down."

Anthony was the first to recover. "Jackie is lucky she has a sister who loves her enough to take action, and bravely tell her parents to wake up. Thank you Jess! Come here, I want to give you a hug. Your Mom and I are sorry we got so involved in what was going on in the company that we lost sight of the most important thing. I hope you will believe me, even if we have not shown it lately, you and your sister mean everything to us. Your welfare comes above all else. Now tell us how long has this been going on with Jackie, and how deeply she is involved with that bad crowd."

"It's really not that long. I think it started a little over two months ago. She started hanging out with this one girl. Her name is Erica. That girl should be one class ahead of us, but she isn't."

"You mean she is older than you and your sister?"

"Yeah, she might even be closer to two years older. Anyway, this Erica girl hangs out with a rough bunch. Most of them don't even go to our school. For the life of me, I can't understand what Jackie sees in Erica. What on earth my sister has in common with that crowd beats me. It wasn't until Jackie started borrowing money from me that I became suspicious drugs might be involved. I did not ask her about it not until after I noticed some of the jewelry grandpa gave us was missing. You know Jackie and I are pretty close, and she never kept secrets from me before. She denied using drugs. We argued and it led to a nasty fight. She hasn't been very nice to me ever since. I really think that you two should have noticed the change in her attitude towards me. How could you miss the changes in her behavior?"

Kay relayed her embrace, "Jessie, if ever a daughter had the right to point out her parents' failure, you have it now. Your father and I have a lot of soul searching to do, but I think right now the first priority is to help Jackie."

Anthony agreed with Kay, "Since you brought it to our attention we owe it to you to listen to you. What would you like us to do?"

"I really don't know; I don't understand it. We have always done everything together, and for no reason I know of she gets involved with those stupid people. Drugs, who in the hell wants to do drugs? Why? There is no reason to take that shit!"

Anthony agreed with her, "Calm down honey. We agree with you that it's stupid to get involved with drugs, but to get angry about it will not help Jackie."

"Dad is right. She needs our support. By being angry with her we risk pushing her further away from us. We'll have to start by talking to her in the morning."

The next morning Anthony cancelled his flight to New York. Immediately after that he called his father-in-law to let him know he had to delay his start in the New York office. Of course, Frank wanted to know why. Anthony knew he had to let his father-in-law know something serious was going on, but at the same time he wanted to protect his daughter. He had not spoken to her yet, and he didn't think it necessary to tell her grandfather exactly what was wrong. "It's Jackie. The kid is having troubles at school, and Kay and I feel it is best I look into it. I'll keep you informed and let you know as soon as possible when I can reschedule my flight."

"Trouble in school? What the hell does that mean? It's got to be pretty serious to keep you in Chicago."

"Yeah, I think it is pretty serious, and Kay was quick to remind me how much she appreciated her Dad's support when she was having trouble."

"Okay wise-guy, I get it. Grandpa lay off, so I won't ask. But remember son, you're only the father. I'm the grandfather. Go take care of the child."

Jackie was not very cooperative the next morning when her parents wanted to talk to her. "I'll be late for school. Can't we talk some other time?"

"I have already called the school to inform them that you'll be late today, and I have cancelled my flight to New York so your mother and I could have some time to talk to you."

"What the hell is this about? Did Jessie tell you some stupid lies about me? Whatever she told you it's not true! She tells all sorts of lies about me because she is jealous. She is angry because my friends hate her. They think she is a fruitcake."

Anthony very calmly asked his daughter to sit down. He sat down next to her on the big leather living room couch, and in a quiet voice said, "Jackie, we haven't said anything yet and already you are getting angry and accusing your sister of lying about you. Why is that? Do you have something to hide?"

"Of course not. She's just upset that I won't hang around with her all the time, and she probably came to you to complain. Don't worry. I know the routine. Be nice to your sister, spend more time with her, and make sure you involve her in things you do."

"Actually, we are glad you did not involve her in the things you do."

"Why not?" Jackie gave Kay a suspicious look but her posture remained defiant.

"Because the people you have been hanging around with are bad. They do bad things and you have participated in those bad things."

"What the hell are you talking about? You don't even know my friends. What bad things are you talking about?"

"Tell us honestly, do those new friends of yours use drugs, and have you used anything?"

Jackie bounced from the couch and as she headed out the room she screamed, "I have had enough of this shit. I have no idea what you're talking about."

"Jackie come back and sit down!!" Jackie stopped in her tracks; she had never heard her father speak so harshly. She slowly returned to the couch, and Anthony continued in a calmer tone.

"Jackie we did not bring you up that way, and we do not accept your being disrespectful to your mother and me. Now, calmly tell us what exactly is going on with you. Be honest with us. Did you or did you not use any type of drugs?"

Jackie looked at her parents. At first it seemed as if she was going to deny using anything. But she changed her mind, "Yeah, I tried some pot to see what it was like. I don't see why you are making such a big deal of it. There's nothing wrong with trying the stuff to see what it's like."

Kay's look at Anthony indicated that she wanted him to answer for both of them. Anthony hesitated for a moment. He wanted to make sure that Jackie was looking directly at him and that he had eye contact with his daughter.

"Jackie you're only fourteen years old. You may feel pretty grown-up, but we feel that there are certain decisions you are too young to make for yourself. That includes the use of drugs, even if it is just to see what it is like. What exactly did you or are you using?"

"Oh it was just some pot, you know, marihuana. A lot of kids at school smoke some marihuana now and then. I really don't see anything wrong in that."

Kay joined in, "Sweetheart, we don't agree with your using that stuff. What other kids do is for their parents to decide, if they even know about it. But for us it is an absolute no, no. Do you understand that?"

"Yes, I understand, but I don't agree. You two are just too old-fashioned to know what most kids are into these days. A lot of people smoke pot, and there is nothing wrong with that. It's better than using alcohol and getting drunk."

Anthony waved off her argument. "Jackie, I am not ready to discuss that issue with you at this time. Enough said. You are fourteen, and we are not letting you decide for yourself that it is all right to smoke pot at your young age. As your parents, we have decided that you will not be allowed to experiment with any type of drug and you will stop. Do I make myself clear?"

"I guess so. But how did you find out? Did Jessie tell you? Why should she be allowed to tell on me?"

"I don't think she really wanted to, but she felt she had to protect you."

"Protect me. That's really ridiculous."

"No it is not. Your sister is very concerned about the crowd you have been hanging around with. It's a bad crowd and certainly not the type of kids you should hang around with."

"Because they sometimes smoke marihuana does not make them bad."

Her exasperation with Jackie's arguments was clearly noticeable in Kay's voice. "Jackie, stop it! You know darn well what we are talking about. In your heart, you know your sister is right. That crowd is not good for you for a lot more reasons than the fact that they use pot. You don't belong there, and you know it."

"Alright already, you don't want me to be friends with those kids. I don't agree, but I'll back off and stop seeing them. Does that make you happy?"

Anthony was not quite sure they had gotten through to Jackie. "It is important for us to be sure you know why we do not want you to smoke pot. Heck, you're not allowed to smoke, no matter what it is. As for being friends with those kids. Okay, maybe we are wrong calling them bad. We just want you to understand why we are uncomfortable with you hanging around with them. Come on Jackie, look at me and tell me you don't know why we don't like for you to hang with that crowd."

Jackie sat quietly for a while, her shoulders slumping forward. "Yes, I get it. I'll stay away from them."

"I have to trust you kiddo. I have to start in the New York office, and I don't want to leave your mother worrying about you and who you are hanging around with."

"Okay, Dad, I'll be okay."

XXXIX

The Board of Directors meeting of Goodman Industries had been going on for twenty minutes when Anthony's secretary burst into the stately conference room. With a signal of his hand Anthony waved her off, but she continued to approach him.

"Sorry, it's an emergency," she breathlessly whispered into his ear.

"Can't it wait till after the meeting?"

"Please, your wife is on the phone; please come with me now!"

Anthony got up and excused himself to the assembled Board Members. "Mr. Chairman, ladies and gentlemen there seems to be an emergency. Please excuse me for a moment, so I can look into something that apparently requires my immediate attention." With that, he hurriedly followed his secretary back to his office. The elevator ride back up to his office on the thirty-first floor seemed to take forever. Once back in his office he grabbed the phone and barked into it "Kay, what's the matter!"

"It's Jackie! She's gone."

"What do you mean gone?"

"She's not here. I can't find her." Kay was sobbing hysterically at the other end.

"Gone from where, when?"

Between sobs Kay related what happened. "When she did not come down for breakfast, I went up to her room to look for her. She was not there, so I checked if Jessie knew where she was. Jessie had no idea. The two of us looked all through the house, but we could not find her. I checked back in her room and her backpack with all her school stuff was still there. Strange, but her cell phone was lying on the bed. It looked like she had just tossed it there. When I checked her bathroom I noticed that some of the toilet articles she uses were missing, and back in her room I saw that some clothing was missing, more than she could be wearing at one time."

"Call the police and report her missing."

"I will as soon as I hang up. Anthony, please come home. I need you here!!"

"I won't wait for a commercial flight. I'll call for them to get the company plane ready to take me to O'Hare."

"Please hurry. Anthony, we have to find her!"

Anthony raced back to the Board Meeting. As soon as he entered the room he addressed the Chairman. "Mr. Chairman, I have a point of order. Please."

Frank Goodman looked at him and quickly said, "The Chair recognizes Mr. Walker."

"Mr. Chairman, I move for an indefinite recess of this meeting." Before anyone could question why he was making this unusual request; Anthony continued, "My daughter is missing, and I have to return to Chicago."

Fred McHennesy, the sour faced Chairman of one of the biggest container transport companies, jumped up. "That is ridiculous. All of us traveled a long way to attend this meeting, and you cannot call an indefinite recess just because Walker cannot find his daughter."

Frank Goodman in a loud voice told him to sit down. "Fred the request was addressed to me. I am the Chairman, and I am adjourning this meeting until further notice."

Fred was not about to give up that easily. "You can't do that! Frank this is not some family club of yours. We cannot meet only when it pleases you and your family."

"Mr. McHennesy, may I remind you that I hold the majority of the voting shares and if you don't watch out you will not be on this Board come next election." With that Frank got up and walked over to Anthony who was waiting for him at the door. "What the hell is going on?"

"Kay called. She is frantic, Jackie is missing."

"Kidnapped?"

"Don't think so. She was home last night, but Kay says she was missing this morning. Kay would have told me if there were signs that she left other than under her own will. As I told you, we were having some trouble with her. I told Kay to call the police and report her missing."

"Don't do that. She is a good child; it will probably turn out to be a big misunderstanding. No need to drag our name all over the news."

"Sorry Dad, not your call. She is my daughter, and I am not about to sit back and let something happen to her." Before his father-in-law could respond, Anthony raced for the elevators on his way to the car waiting downstairs to take him to the airport.

The plane ride seemed to take forever and Anthony went up front to ask the pilots if they could speed up.

"Sorry Boss, can't do. But I have good news for you. We have permission to land on a runway which gives us direct access to an area where a car will be waiting on the tarmac to take you straight to your house."

"Thanks for arranging that for me." To calm his nerves Anthony lingered in the cockpit to chat with the pilots.

Kay and Jessie were standing at the front door when Anthony's car pulled up to the house. It was obvious both had been crying. Anthony tried to calm them down by repeatedly assuring them everything would be okay and they would find Jackie very soon. Jessie was not convinced. She blamed herself for not keeping a more careful eye on her sister.

"I just knew that she did not mean it when she told you she was through with those kids. She is angry you told her to stop seeing them. She has probably run off to be with them. I bet those bastards know where my sister is. Daddy, you have to go after them. I am sure Jackie is with them. Oh, I'm so sorry. It's my fault. I should have stopped her. How could I not notice what she was planning? How in the world did she leave the house without me hearing? We sleep in adjoining bedrooms!"

Kay put her arms around Jessie's shoulders. "Stop blaming yourself. It's not your fault. If anyone should have been watching her more carefully it is I. As her mother I should have known she did not mean it when she said she was through with those kids."

Anthony had heard enough, "Will you two please stop it. Nobody is to blame here. Jackie isn't a liar. I am sure she meant it when she said she would stop seeing those kids. Something happened in the last few days to change that. I have no idea what that can be. But to find out we have to ask that girl Erica, the one she was hanging out with."

"I could help with that." Jessie said.

"Absolutely not" Anthony was adamant. Jessie should under no circumstances approach Erica or for that matter anyone else in the group. "That is something we should not do ourselves. I am going down to see the police right now to ask them to question that girl."

Since Anthony did not know Erica's last name or her address, the police went to the school to try and speak to her. Erica was not in school, and the school's principal went with them to her house. Nobody was home, and the police had a lot of trouble locating Erica's parents. When they finally located Erica's mother, they learned Erica had not been home for several days. Her mother said she had been staying at a friend's house, but the mother had no idea who this friend was. According to the mother, this was not unusual. Erica often stayed with friends.

The police returned to the school, and questioned all the kids who were pointed out to them as friends of Erica. Not one of them had any idea where Erica could be found. The police seemed to indicate that their investigation had reached a dead-end and from then on they would have to rely on tips coming in from the public. They tried to assure Anthony that somebody would report having seen Jackie. A missing persons report, containing her picture, had been widely circulated.

Given Anthony's prominent position as C.E.O. of Goodman Industries, the story was being covered in the national news programs. To make sure they were not dealing with a kidnapping, the police made a thorough investigation of the Walker home to see if there was any indication Jackie had been taken forcefully from her home. Given the wealth of her grandfather this was still something they wanted to consider, although the apparent connection with Erica's disappearance made this unlikely.

During the next two days, Kay and Anthony became more and more frightened. It did not help any that Kay's parents called every few hours to ask if there was any news about Jackie. Kay's mother kept praying that Jackie would show up at her front door. "I am so close to that child, she'll come to me." She somehow managed to get on CBS News with a personal plea for Jackie to call her. She would come get her, no questions asked no matter where she was or why she left. Kay and Anthony were searching closer to home. In separate cars they searched the city, but they could not come up with a single clue. Anthony was about to hire an army of private detectives to help in the search when he received a call from Jamal.

"I'm on the way."

"Thanks, but I don't know what you can do to help. I think I'll hire some private detectives to help in the search. How did you find out?"

"It's all over the news. You should have called me."

"Yeah, but what can you do in this situation?"

"Anthony, you're my best friend. When you have a horrible problem like this, Valerie and I have to be there to support you and Kay."

"What about your kids?"

"That's what mothers-in-law are for. She is on her way. We'll leave as soon as she gets here."

XL

Valerie's arrival had a calming effect on Kay. Although she could not actually do anything to help find Jackie, it did give Kay a strong person to lean on while Anthony and Jamal were working the phones, trying to enlist people they knew to help find Jackie. Valerie also made sure that Jessie was not forgotten. She kept reminding Kay that the kid was also scared and needed her mother more than ever.

After a full day of working the phones, Jamal took Anthony aside. "Look, we're getting nowhere this way. I need more information. Tell me more details about the days before Jackie disappeared. Was there anything else besides you telling her not to hang around with that girl Erica?"

"Well it all started with Jennie telling us that the crowd Jackie had started hanging around with smoked pot."

"Did she suspect that Jackie was using?"

"Yes she did."

"Why?"

"Jackie had borrowed money from her and she noticed that some of their jewelry was missing."

"Okay, we are finally getting somewhere."

"What do you mean?"

"You're forgetting that I'm a kid who grew up in the hood and spent a long time in the NBA. I have learned you always follow the drug trail. You'd be amazed what we'll find out." Jamal went on to explain that the clue was not that she had probably smoked some pot. What was important was that she buying the stuff and there had been some contact between her and a seller. She could still be in contact with this supplier. He suggested they go see one of his friends, Ricky Johansen, who still played for the Chicago Bulls. Although this guy probably did not use anything that might affect his playing, he probably would know a lot about the current drug scene in Chicago.

Ricky proved to be a wealth of information. They came away with a long list of people who could have sold Jackie some marijuana. One name stood out, Scooter Barnes. Scooter had been a highly recruited college basketball star, but he had been dropped from the Bulls' team in his rookie year because of his extensive involvement with drugs. Ricky had given them Scooter's address. Anthony and Jamal went to see him.

Scooter made no effort to hide the fact that he was involved in selling marijuana, but he assured them he did not know Jackie. As a matter of fact he insisted he never sold any drugs to minors, and he had no intention of getting involved in that sort of trade. Anthony thought they had hit another dead end but as they were leaving Scooter said.

"I didn't sell the kid any stuff, but I can get you some information."

"What do you mean by that?" Jamal asked.

"Like I said, I can get you some information. Maybe even find out where the girl is hanging out."

"When can you get that information?"

"That depends on the gratitude your friend here shows."

Jamal had no trouble understanding what Scooter meant. "How much gratitude have you got in mind?"

"Five thousand if I come up with some useable information. Ten thousand, if I tell you exactly where she can be found."

Before Jamal had a chance to respond, Anthony said, "You've got a deal. I'll have the cash ready."

XLI

Each time the phone rang, everybody froze. Could this be Scooter calling? Kay had already given up hope. "He was just bluffing. If the police can't find her he certainly can't."

Jamal thought she was wrong. "Don't be so sure. Those shady characters are all somehow connected. I think he will call with something. He would not have offered to help if he did not need the money. And money speaks loudly in his circles. He won't be able to keep much of it; there will be many separate pay-offs along the way."

Jamal was right. Scooter finally called. "I have the address where the girls are."

"Wonderful, where is that?"

"Not so fast. First the money. Then I give you the address."

Anthony's hands were shaking as he signaled thumbs- up to Kay who was holding on to Valerie and Jessie as if her life depended on it. He tried to control his voice as best he could.

"Agreed, where do we meet?"

"I am sitting in a black suburban parked just down the street from your house. It looks like a cop car is parked in front of your house. So send Jamal to bring me the cash, and I'll give him the address."

Anthony handed the envelope with ten thousand dollars to Jamal and told him Scooter was waiting for him in a black suburban.

Jamal took the envelope and started for the door. He stopped and turned to Anthony.

"You realize this could be a trick, and she is not at the address he gives us."

"I am fully aware of that, but my daughter is worth much more than the money we could lose. I'll gladly take the chance."

Jamal was back in less than ten minutes.

"I have the address. It's an apartment on South Woodlawn. It belongs to a couple who are rumored to take-in runaway girls, and hide them from their parents and authorities. According to Scooter we are just in time. This couple's intentions are not good. The girls who windup there have no idea what they are in for. Scooter recommends we call the police to meet us there, and not go in until after they have raided the place. Scooter says he is a boy scout compared to the despicable work this couple is engaged in. If the police promise to keep him out of it, he is willing to supply enough evidence to put this couple away for a long time."

"You mean sex trade?" Kay cried out.

"Yes". Jamal said. "Thank God we are in time. Scooter says both girls are still okay. Now let me call the police to meet us there."

The police arrived in full force. Three squad cars pulled up in front of the building, and several policemen rushed to surround the building. When they had all outside doors covered, the Swat Team filed out of their van and headed for the targeted apartment. The officer in charge of the operation instructed Anthony and Jamal to take cover in one of the squad cars until he gave them the okay to go up to the apartment.

The entire operation took less than seven minutes. The Swat Team raced up the stairs, and identified themselves as police. When nobody opened the door, they broke it down and entered the apartment. At first they saw nothing but an empty apartment, but when they searched the place they found four men and a woman in one of the bedrooms. In another bedroom they found six girls huddled together. The girls had heard the police enter, and were scared because they were discovered. All six were run-aways, ranging in age from twelve to seventeen. The officer in charge told the adults they were under arrest on suspicion of slave trafficking with the intent to sell the girls into prostitution.

After the five adults had been led away, Anthony and Jamal were allowed to come up to the apartment. The girls had heard why the five adults were arrested, and Sergeant Kitty Hernandez, from the juvenile division, quickly went over to them to assure them that they were safe. They had done nothing wrong, and the police were there to take them home. When Jackie saw her father she ran to him.

"Daddy I'm so sorry. You're very angry with me, aren't you?"

"No, honey, I'm not angry. All I want to do is hold you tight and take you home to your mother."

"I can't go home. I'm different! You and Mom won't like it."

Anthony was puzzled. He had no idea what Jackie was talking about. He put down his cell phone which he taken out to call Kay to tell her Jackie was all right, and they were on their way home.

"What in the world does that mean? Of course we can go home."

"You don't understand. I am different." She turned away from Anthony and sobbed. "I am different. I like girls."

Without any hesitation Anthony replied, "So what?"

Jackie looked at him, surprised by his reaction. "You're okay with that? That doesn't make you're angry?"

"Why in the world should that make me angry? You are my daughter, and if that is the way you feel, so be it. It certainly does not make me love you less. Come here and let me give you a big hug." Anthony could no longer hold back the emotions he had tried to suppress while Jackie was missing. He squeezed his daughter in his arms while the tears flowed down his cheeks. Between sobs he whispered. "Baby, I've been so scared. I missed you so very much." He calmed down when Jamal tapped him on the shoulder.

"Time to go home. I have already called Kay to tell her all is well and we are on our way home."

As they were leaving the apartment, they could clearly hear Erica arguing with Sergeant Hernandez.

"This is all Bull Shit! You have no right barging in here and taking us away. These people have done nothing wrong. You're lying! They won't hurt us. We're staying here because we want to. You're just doing this to break up Jackie and me. It won't work. We love each other. Jackie won't leave me!"

The outburst did not seem to bother Kitty Hernandez. "Sorry young lady, you girls are minors, and it is our duty to take you home. Jackie is going home with her Dad. You and the other girls are coming with me. It will be easier for all of us if you calm down and cooperate with me."

During the ride home, Jackie asked, "What about Mom? Will she accept that I'm not like other girls? That I am gay."

"You just heard Uncle Jamal tell you that he knows women who have feelings for other women and it doesn't affect his friendship with them in any way. So why do you think your mother won't accept it?"

"I don't know, but I'm scared about it. You two are guys and I think men can more easily accept two women liking each other than a woman can. What about two men? Do you accept two men liking each other?"

"That's a very grown-up question," Jamal said. "I don't think it depends on if you're a man or a woman. I am not going to lie to you. Some people have a real problem accepting folks who are gay. An ex-team mate of mine, we played on the same team for five years, did not admit he was gay until after he retired. When I asked him why he kept it a secret for all those years, he told me he was sure he'd be dropped from the team if he told anyone. When I told him I didn't think that would have happened, he tried to explain why he felt he had to hide his true feelings for all those years. We argued about it but he insisted that unless you are guy yourself you cannot understand the difficulties he faced. So Jackie, I want you to keep talking to your parents about your true feelings. Those of us who love you will be there to make sure you'll never have to hide from who you are."

Jackie got out of the car very slowly. Anthony had assured her that everything would be all right, but she was still very scared to face her mother. She clutched her father's hand as they approached the house. The front door flew open and Kay come racing down the steps. She threw her arms around Jackie, and Jackie burrowed her head in her mother's chest. They silently held on to each other until Jackie looked up at her mother. "I'm sorry Mom. Oh Mommy, I'm so sorry."

Kay squeezed her daughter even tighter in her arms. "I don't know sorry, I only know I love you."

Jackie had trouble breathing her mother held her so tightly.

"Baby you're home. Thank God you' re home."

Tears of joy were flowing freely when the two of them walk into the house.

When things had calmed down Jackie said, "Mom there is something Daddy has to tell you. There is a reason why I ran away."

Anthony objected, "Why not tell her yourself?"

"Please Daddy, I can't. Please help me and explain it to Mom."

Anthony made sure it did not sound like a big deal when he said, "She's trying to tell you she is gay."

Kay looked at her daughter. "And that's the reason you ran from us? But honey you can't do anything about that. You did nothing wrong. Why run away?"

"I thought you'd be mad at me."

"Sweetheart, that isn't something you have to be ashamed of and hide from us. You can't control that. Of course we are not mad at you. I thought you left because we were mad you smoked pot."

"No, that was not the reason. I did not know how to tell you. We never discussed that sort of thing. I did not know if you could accept the idea of my being gay. You can't be happy about it!"

"Of course we are not happy about it. But that is more for you than for us. It will make your life more difficult. In some ways you'll be different from other girls, and that will be very hard for you. Not everybody will accept you for who you are. But we are your parents. Our love comes without qualifications. I hope you fully understand that."

Jessie had been noticeably quite during the long family reunion. After the girls had gone to bed, Jackie opened the connecting door and went into Jessie's bedroom.

"You're mad at me aren't you?"

"Yes." Jessie answered curtly.

"But why? Don't you understand that I can't help the way I am? I am not doing this on purpose. You heard Mom and Dad explain that."

"It's not that at all."

"Then what the hell is wrong. Why are you mad at me?"

"You could have told me! Why did you lock me out? We never had secrets before; we used to tell each other everything. And now with something really important, you did not trust me. Damn you. You could have told me. I am your sister!"

"I didn't think you would understand."

"Why wouldn't I understand?"

"The way you reacted when we watched a T.V. movie, and in it two of the women kissed. They were lovers and you said that was ridiculous. When I tried to defend them, you made a nasty remark about them. You called them stupid lesbians."

Jessie's face looked like she had seen a ghost. "Oh my God! I remember. We argued about it, and I said those stupid things. Jackie I am sorry. I argued with you because it was a pretty stupid movie, and I did not like those two women. I called them stupid lesbians, not because I think lesbians are stupid, but because those two characters were stupid. I found the whole love scene rather silly. If I had known how you felt, I would have realized that scene touched you in a personal way and that's why you defended them. Jackie, to me it was just a silly movie, but now I understand what a horrible thing I did. Will this drive us apart?"

"Can you accept that I am gay?"

Jessie ran to her, "Jackie I want my sister back. I don't care if you walk upside down, you are my best friend. Don't ever lock me out again."

"Okay, I promise no more secrets."

Jessie's habitual good-humor returned almost instantly, "At least we won't be fighting over the same boy."

Jackie was not ready to see the humor in the situation. "Yeah, but what will you do if some girls refuse to be friends with us because they know about me?"

"I wouldn't worry about that. We probably wouldn't want to friends with them either."

XLII

To help his family settle back into their regular routine, Anthony postponed his return to New York for a few extra days. To prove to Jackie that she had regained their complete trust Anthony and Kay decided that it would be best for her to go back to school as soon as possible. This proved to be a big mistake. On the very first day Jackie came storming back into the house.

"No way am I ever going back to that school. Never again!!"

Kay came rushing from the kitchen, "What's the matter honey? What happened?"

"My picture was all over the news, and everybody saw the posters. They all know why I ran away, and they were making fun of me. One of the older boys pointed me out and called me Erica's bitch, and all his friends laughed." Kay immediately called Anthony to come hear what happened.

Both parents were trying to console their daughter when Jessie walked into the room. Anthony saw that she looked a little disheveled and her hair was messed-up. "Did you come home with Jackie?"

"Yeah, we walked home together. They're all a bunch of ass-holes; they are stupid, stupid, all of them!! Especially Barbara, she's really an idiot."

"You mean your friend Barbara Sieverts?"

"I should have hit her a lot harder than I did. She made fun of Jackie behind her back and then asked me if Jackie was still allowed to sleep in the same room as me. I punched her, and we got into a big fight. The teacher broke it up, and because she did not know what that stupid Barbara said, she blamed me for starting the fight."

Anthony had to suppress a smile, he was proud of Jessie for sticking up for her sister. But his thoughts were quickly interrupted by Jackie's angry outburst.

"Why did you have to spread my name all over town? For God's sake you even gave my picture to the news."

Kay started to answer but did not know where to begin. She was groping for the proper words and looked at Anthony for help. He tried to explain.

"To go public about something so deeply personal as having a missing child is certainly about the last thing parents want to do. But we were in total panic and felt we had no choice. We were desperately afraid. You were out there all by yourself, and we feared that you were in danger. We love you and we were scared. We were ready to do anything if it would help bring you home safely. That included going to the police and asking them to make a missing person report."

"Daddy you just don't know how awful it is to have your name all over the news and everybody knowing that I ran away, some even know why."

"Baby, I know. I truly know and I feel your pain."

"How could you possibly know!"

Kay shot Anthony an anxious look but Anthony shook his head as to say "not now," and he continued. "Maybe we can discuss that when you're a little older, but for now you have your parents to support you through a very difficult time. Together we will get through this. You're lucky. Besides your Mother and me, you have a sister who has your back no matter what."

XLIII

The school year was about to end in a few weeks, and since the family was moving to New York, the principal readily agreed that the girls did not have to return to school. Anthony had already made arrangements to lease a renovated brownstone on West Ninetieth Street in the city, and for the next school year the girls were already enrolled in a mid-town private school. Kay planned to stay in Chicago to sell the house and make arrangements for the move. In the meantime, the girls were going to stay with their grandparents.

Jackie was worried about her grandparents' reaction to her having come out as being gay.

"Mom did you tell them about me?"

"Of course, honey. Remember we agreed not to make a secret out of it."

"Yeah I know. But how did they react?"

"When I told Grandma she was very surprised, but she finally understood why you had run away.

She seemed very concerned about your reaction, and we did not really go into her feelings about it."

"But can she accept it?"

"Of course she can."

"How can you be so sure of that?"

"Jackie, dear, she's my Mother. She brought me up and instilled her values in me. Believe me, I know. She adores her two granddaughters, and nothing is going to change that."

"What about Grandpa? Have you spoken to him?"

"No I haven't, but if he has any qualms about it, he'll have to deal with your grandmother. Believe me, with Grandma on your side you have nothing to worry about. But when you get to Jersey, I want you to openly discuss it with your grandfather."

The day after she arrived at her grandparents' house, Jackie opened the subject at breakfast.

"Grandpa, do you think it is strange that I am not like other girls?"

Frank looked at his granddaughter and smiled.

"I was hoping to discuss that with you. By asking, you have made it easier for me. I have to go into my office to make some calls, but if you will be my date I'd like to take you to lunch at the club so we can talk, just the two of us. Jessie, you don't mind do you that I just take Jackie?"

"I don't mind. She'll tell me everything anyway. We have no secrets from each other."

When they walked into the dining room at the country club, Frank said to Jackie. "Some of the men are staring at us, and they are jealous as hell. Can't say I blame them; you and your sister are beautiful young ladies. The two of you make me very proud, and I love to be seen with you."

That was a good lead-in for the discussion Frank wanted to have with his granddaughter. "You have the right to know how I feel about having a granddaughter who is gay and, I will try to explain my feelings. I am of an older generation, and when I grew up my parents would not have been able to accept it. The whole idea of someone being gay was strange to me. I had to adjust to it as I was growing up. Sure, along the way I met some people who were gay, but it was not until I got to college that I had friends who were gay. After I got to know them, I liked them. The fact that they were gay was no longer a big deal.

"The same thing happened when I first met your father. Your mother announced she was bringing home a boy she really liked and she was anxious for us to meet him. That sounded pretty serious, and we were happy she apparently had a boyfriend. But to be honest I had serious reservations about this fellow. Your mother had told us he was on the wrestling team and on full scholarship. That made me suspect he was probably none too bright, and that the university had admitted him for his athletic ability, not for his scholastic achievements. Besides, he had grown up in a tough section of New York City, and had been in some serious trouble. I really doubted he was a good match for my daughter. When he walked in, tall and very handsome, I was sure my daughter was somewhat star struck by this captain of the wrestling team, but that their romance would not last very long. I even entertained the thought that this guy might have an eye on our money.

"The first night of their stay, after everybody had gone to bed, I had a chance to have a long talk with this fellow. Guess what? I really liked him. This was not some shallow athlete. I discovered he was a very intelligent young man, and I enjoyed talking to him. Later when I already knew I liked him quite a bit, I learned my suspicion that he might be after your Mom's money was totally unfounded. On the contrary, he nearly shied away from us because of it. I learned to love this man. He turned out to be everything a man could wish for in a son-in-law.

"Now why am I telling you this about your father? The point I am trying to make is you really have to know someone before making a judgment about them. You know I'm crazy about you. So when your grandmother told me you had told your parents you were gay, I was very surprised, but I was able to put it in the context of the person you are. I love you, and now that I know your feelings about your sexuality I accept it as part of who you are, but it will never be the major part. You and I both know, some people just won't accept you because you are gay. That maybe because of their religious belief, or because of what their parents taught them. We can't change that. They are entitled to their viewpoint, but if they do anything or say anything that harms you they'll have me to deal with."

Jackie reached across the table for her grandfather's hand. "Gee Grandpa, you're the best. But you don't have to worry about me. I have the greatest parents in the world and they will always stand by me and protect me.

CPSIA information can be obtained at www.ICGtesting.com
Printed in the USA
LVOW04s2128250515

439714LV00023B/537/P